William Shakespeare's Timon of Athens: A Retelling in Prose

David Bruce

Published by David Bruce, 2022.

WILLIAM SHAKESPEARE'S TIMON OF ATHENS: A RETELLING IN PROSE

First edition. July 28, 2022.

ISBN: 979-8201210762

Written by David Bruce.

Table of Contents

Dedication

Dedicated to Carl Eugene Bruce and Josephine Saturday Bruce

My father, Carl Eugene Bruce, died on 24 October 2013. He used to work for Ohio Power, and at one time, his job was to shut off the electricity of people who had not paid their bills. He sometimes would find a home with an impoverished mother and some children. Instead of shutting off their electricity, he would tell the mother that she needed to pay her bill or soon her electricity would be shut off. He would write on a form that no one was home when he stopped by because if no one was home he did not have to shut off their electricity.

The best good deed that anyone ever did for my father occurred after a storm that knocked down many power lines. He and other linemen worked long hours and got wet and cold. Their feet were freezing because water got into their boots and soaked their socks. Fortunately, a kind woman gave my father and the other linemen dry socks to wear.

My mother, Josephine Saturday Bruce, died on 14 June 2003. She used to work at a store that sold clothing. One day, an impoverished mother with a baby clothed in rags walked into the store and started shoplifting in an interesting way: The mother took the rags off her baby and dressed the infant in new clothing. My mother knew that this mother could not afford to buy the clothing, but she helped the mother dress her baby and then she watched as the mother walked out of the store without paying.

***

The doing of good deeds is important. As a free person, you can choose to live your life as a good person or as a bad person. To be a good person, do good deeds. To be a bad person, do bad deeds. If you do good deeds, you will become good. If you do bad deeds, you will become bad. To become the person you want to be, act as if you already are that kind of person. Each of us chooses what kind of person we will become. To become a good person, do the things a good person does. To become a bad person, do the things a bad person does. The opportunity to take action to become the kind of person you want to be is yours.

Human beings have free will. According to the Babylonian Niddah 16b, whenever a baby is to be conceived, the Lailah (angel in charge of contraception) takes the drop of semen that will result in the conception and asks God, "Sovereign of the Universe, what is going to be the fate of this drop? Will it develop into a robust or into a weak person? An intelligent or a stupid person? A wealthy or a poor person?" The Lailah asks all these questions, but it does not ask, "Will it develop into a righteous or a wicked person?" The answer to that question lies in the decisions to be freely made by the human being that is the result of the conception.

A Buddhist monk visiting a class wrote this on the chalkboard: "EVERYONE WANTS TO SAVE THE WORLD, BUT NO ONE WANTS TO HELP MOM DO THE DISHES." The students laughed, but the monk then said, "Statistically, it's highly unlikely that any of you will ever have the opportunity to run into a burning orphanage and rescue an infant. But, in the smallest gesture of kindness — a warm smile, holding the door for the person behind you, shoveling the driveway of the elderly person next door — you have committed an act of immeasurable profundity, because to each of us, our life is our universe."

In her book titled *I Have Chosen to Stay and Fight*, comedian Margaret Cho writes, "I believe that we get complimentary snack-size portions of the afterlife, and we all receive them in a different way." For Ms. Cho, many of her snack-size portions of the afterlife come in hip hop music. Other people get different snack-size portions of the afterlife, and we all must be on the lookout for them when they come our way. And perhaps doing good deeds and experiencing good deeds are snack-size portions of the afterlife.

***

In this retelling, as in all my retellings, I have tried to make the work of literature accessible to modern readers who may lack the knowledge about mythology, religion, and history that the literary work's contemporary audience had.

Do you know a language other than English? If you do, I give you permission to translate this book, copyright your translation, publish or self-publish it, and keep all the royalties for yourself. (Do give me credit, of course, for the original retelling.)

I would like to see my retellings of classic literature used in schools, so I give permission to the country of Finland (and all other countries) to give copies of this book to all students forever. I also give permission to the state of Texas (and all other states) to give copies of this book to all students forever. I also give permission to all teachers to give copies of this book to all students forever.

Teachers need not actually teach my retellings. Teachers are welcome to give students copies of my eBooks as background material. For example, if they are teaching Homer's *Iliad* and *Odyssey*, teachers are welcome to give students copies of my *Virgil's* Aeneid: *A Retelling in Prose* and tell students, "Here's another ancient epic you may want to read in your spare time."

CAST OF CHARACTERS

Male Characters

Timon of Athens.

Lucius, Lucullus, Sempronius, flattering Lords.

Ventidius, one of Timon's false friends.

Apemantus, a churlish Cynic philosopher.

Alcibiades, an Athenian Captain.

Poet, Painter, Jeweler, Merchant.

Certain Senators.

Certain Masquers (Ladies dressed as Amazons).

Certain Thieves.

Flavius, steward to Timon.

Flaminius, Lucilius, Servilius, servants to Timon.

Caphis, Philotus, Titus, Lucius, Hortensius, several servants to Usurers and to the Lords.

Female Characters

Phrygia, Timandra, mistresses to Alcibiades.

Minor Characters

Cupid.

Diverse other Servants and Attendants.

Servants of Ventidius and of Varro and Isidore (two of Timon's Creditors).

Three Strangers.

An Old Athenian.

A Page.

A Fool.

Scene

Athens, and the neighboring Woods.

CHAPTER 1

— 1.1 —

In a hall in Timon's house, several people stood. A poet and a painter stood together, and a jeweler and a merchant stood together.

The poet said to the painter, "Good day, sir."

"I am glad you're well," the painter replied.

"I have not seen you for a long time. How goes the world?"

"How goes the world?" was a way of saying, "How are you?" However, the painter took the question literally.

"It wears, sir, as it grows," the painter replied. "The world wears out as it grows older. With entropy, someday the world will wear out completely."

"Yes, that's well known," the poet said, "but what particular rarity do we see in the world? What strange event never experienced before and without equal — according to many and varied witnesses and records of history — do we see?"

The poet answered his own question: "See the magic of bounty and generosity! The power of bounty and generosity has conjured all these spirits to be in attendance here and now."

He was referring to the people present, all of whom were present because of Timon's bounty. Timon was a very generous man.

The poet pointed and said, "I know that merchant."

"I know both of the men," the painter said. "The other man's a jeweler."

A short distance away, the merchant said, "Oh, he is a worthy lord."

The jeweler replied, "That's very certain."

"He is a very incomparable man, and he keeps his generosity well exercised. His goodness is, as it were, tireless and enduring. He is surpassingly generous."

The jeweler said, "I have a jewel here —"

"Please, let me see it," the merchant requested. "Is it for the Lord Timon, sir?"

"If he will pay me its estimated value, but as for that —"

As for that, Timon always paid its estimated value.

The poet recited two verses to himself, "*When we for recompense have praised the vile, / it stains the glory in that happy verse that aptly sings the good.*"

A person can praise things that are bad in order to receive money, but doing that devalues praise for things that are good.

Now, lots of praise began to be stated for things for which people were hoping to receive money.

"The jewel is of good quality," the merchant said.

"The quality is rich," the jeweler said. "Look at its luster."

A short distance away, the painter said to the poet, "You are rapt, sir, in some work, some dedication to the great lord."

The great lord was the generous Timon. Poets would often dedicate a work to a generous lord in return for financial patronage.

"These two verses slipped idly and casually from me," the poet said. "Our poetry is similar to gum that oozes from the tree from whence it is nourished."

The poet believed that poetry was easy to write as long as it was nourished — paid for.

The poet added, "The fire in the flint does not show itself until the flint is struck."

There is a way to strike the flint that is this poet so that it produces the spark of poetry. That way is to give this poet money.

The poet continued, "Our refined flame produces itself and like the current flies each barrier it chafes."

According to the poet, writing poetry could be compared to flowing water that went around or leapt over barriers in the stream and then continued downstream.

One can wonder whether truly good poetry can be *easily* written in return for money.

Seeing the painter holding something, the poet asked, "What do you have there?"

"A picture, sir," the painter said. "When does your book come forth?"

"Upon the heels of my presentment, sir."

The poet was present to present his book to Timon; he was fully confident that Timon would approve of the book and would give him money for its publication — and for its composition.

The poet requested, "Let's see your piece."

Showing the poet his picture, the painter said, "It is a good piece."

"So it is," the poet said. "This picture turned out well, and it is excellent."

"It is indifferent," the painter said.

One can wonder whether the painter was being falsely modest in order to get a compliment, or was telling the truth.

"It is admirable," the poet said about the painting, which depicted a man. "Look at how the gracefulness of this figure proclaims his status! What a mental power this eye shoots forth! How forcefully imagination moves in this lip! The figure is dumb — silent — but the viewer can provide words for the gesture the figure is making."

"It is a pretty mocking of the life," the painter said. "It is a good imitation of reality. Look here at this part. Is it good?"

"I will say about your picture that it tutors nature," the poet said. "Artificial strife lives in these touches that are livelier than life."

The artificial strife was the effort needed to make art. The poet had said that writing poetry was easy when the poetry would be paid for, but to him painting was hard.

Senators now entered the hall and walked in front of the poet and the painter.

"How this lord is followed!" the painter said. "Lots of important people seek his patronage."

"The Senators of Athens seek Timon's patronage!" the poet said. "Timon is a happy man!"

"Look, more are coming!" the painter said.

"You see this confluence, this great flood of visitors," the poet said. "I have, in this rough work, shaped out a man, whom this Earthly world that is below him embraces and hugs with the amplest reception. My free drift halts not particularly, but moves itself in a wide sea of wax: No targeted malice infects one comma in the course I hold; the course I hold flies an eagle flight, bold and straight on, leaving no trace behind."

The poet was describing the work of art that he would present to Timon. It was a work about a man whom many people praised. He did not name any particular man. In addition, he claimed that no maliciousness against any particular person could be discerned in his writing. The scope of the poet's writing was broad. At this time, people often wrote on wax tablets with a stylus, but the poet wrote on a sea of wax — a very broad scope. The poet also claimed that the targeted malice of his writing flew like an eagle; it flew high and straight and left no trace of its passage behind.

In other words, the message of the writing was universal, but it definitely applied to a particular individual. However, the poet expected that his writing would fly over the head of its audience and leave no trace behind.

The poet's words were vague, and the painter said, "How shall I understand you? What are you saying?"

"I will unfold my meaning to you," the poet said. "You see how all social ranks, how all minds, as well of glib and slippery creatures as of grave and austere quality, tender their services to Lord Timon. His large fortune, in conjunction with his good and gracious nature, subdues and appropriates to his love and attention all sorts of hearts. Yes, hearts ranging from those of the mirror-faced flatterers who reflect back the flatteree's own moods and opinions to the Cynic philosopher Apemantus, who loves few things better than to hate himself."

If what the poet said is true, then Apemantus hates himself simply because he is a human being.

The poet continued, "Even Apemantus drops down to his knee when he is before Timon, and returns home happy when Timon acknowledges him by nodding to him."

"I saw them speak together," the painter said.

"Sir, I have represented in my work Lady Fortune, who is enthroned upon a high and pleasant hill. The base of the mountain is surrounded by rows of men with differing degrees of merit and differing kinds of character. These men labor on the bosom of this sphere to increase their wealth. Among them all, whose eyes are fixed on this sovereign lady — Lady Fortune — is one man I describe as being like Lord Timon in disposition and build, whom Lady Fortune with her ivory hand beckons to her. Lord Timon's present grace translates his rivals to present slaves and servants — his ever-present generosity immediately changes his rivals into his slaves and servants."

"You have hit your target," the painter said. "This throne, Lady Fortune, and this hill, in my opinion, with one man beckoned to climb from the rest below, bowing his head against the steep mountain to climb to his happiness, would be well expressed in our condition."

The painter meant that Lady Fortune also beckons creative people such as himself and the poet to climb the mountain. Such a climb is steep, but it is rewarding.

"Sir, continue to listen to me," the poet said. "All those who were his equals just recently, some of whom are worth more than he himself is, at the moment follow his strides, fill his lobbies as if they were his servants and attendants, rain sacrificial whisperings — like the adoring prayers of a priest at a sacrifice — in his ear, treat as a sacred object even his stirrup that they hold as he mounts his horse, and act as if only through him are they able to drink in the air that is free to all."

"What about all these people?" the painter asked.

"When Lady Fortune in her shift and change of mood kicks down her late beloved, all his parasites who labored on their hands and knees and crawled after him to reach the mountain's top now let him slip down the mountain. Not even one will accompany him in his decline."

"That is a commonplace idea," the painter said. "I can show you a thousand moralistic paintings that demonstrate these quick blows of Lady Fortune more pregnantly than words can. Yet you do well to show Lord Timon that lowly eyes have seen the foot above the head."

The eyes of the lowly have seen Lady Fortune's foot above their head just before it kicked them down the steep hill; previously, the eyes of the now lowly were the eyes of the then great.

Trumpets sounded; someone important was coming.

Timon entered the hall and talked courteously with those present — people who had a request to make of him.

A messenger from Ventidius began talking with Timon; Lucilius and other servants followed Timon.

Timon said, "Imprisoned is he, do you say?"

The messenger from Ventidius replied, "Yes, my good lord. Five talents is his debt; his means of repayment are very short, and his creditors are very strict. He wants you to write an honorable letter to those who have shut him up. If you fail to do that, his comfort will come to an end."

The honorable letter would state that Timon would honor — pay — the debt of his friend.

"Noble Ventidius!" Timon said. "Well, I am not of that feather — that kind of person — to shake off my friend when he needs me. I know him to be a gentleman who well deserves help, which he shall have. I'll pay the debt, and free him."

"Your lordship binds Ventidius to you forever with your generosity," the messenger said.

"Convey my greetings to him," Timon said. "I will send his ransom. Once he has been freed, ask him to come to me. It is not enough just to help the feeble up, for we ought to support him afterward. Fare you well."

"All happiness to your honor!" the messenger said as he exited.

An old Athenian man entered the hall and said, "Lord Timon, hear me speak."

"Speak freely, good father," Timon said.

In this society, old men one was not related to were called "father" as a term of respect.

"You have a servant named Lucilius," the old Athenian man said.

"I have," Timon said. "What about him?"

"Most noble Timon, call the man before you."

"Is he here, or not?" Timon asked. "Lucilius!"

"Here I am, at your lordship's service."

"This fellow here, Lord Timon, this creature of yours, by night frequents my house," the old Athenian man said.

The terms "fellow" and "creature" were contemptuous. The old Athenian man looked down on Lucilius because he was a servant and lacked wealth.

The old Athenian man continued, "I am a man who from my first years has been inclined to be thrifty, and my estate deserves an heir more raised than one who holds a trencher."

A trencher is a wooden plate that holds food. Lucilius was a servant who waited on Timon during meals. The old Athenian man's problem with Lucilius courting his daughter was Lucilius' lack of social status and wealth. He wanted his daughter to marry someone with a higher social status and more wealth.

"Well, what further do you have to say?" Timon asked.

"I have only one daughter, no kin else, on whom I may confer what I have gotten throughout my life. The maiden is beautiful and has just become old enough to be a bride, and I have raised her at a very dear cost to have the best accomplishments. This man of yours wants her to be his. I ask you, noble lord, to join with me to forbid him from being in her presence. I myself have spoken to him, but in vain."

"Lucilius is honest," Timon said. "He is honorable and worthy."

"If he is honest, then therefore he will be honest," the old Athenian man replied. "He can show that he is honest by leaving my daughter alone. His honesty will be his reward; his reward must not be my daughter — he must not bear her away."

"Does she love him?" Timon asked.

"She is young and apt — she is impressionable. Our own former passionate feelings teach us what levity's in youth."

Some of the old Athenian man's words had a double meaning. "Apt" could mean "impressionable" or "sexually inclined." "Levity" could mean "frivolity" or "licentiousness." A woman with light heels is a promiscuous woman.

Timon asked Lucilius, "Do you love the maiden?"

"Yes, my good lord, and she accepts my love."

The old Athenian man said, "I call the gods to witness that if in her marriage my consent is missing, I will choose my heir from among the beggars of the world, and dispossess her of all she would have inherited if she had married with my consent."

"How shall she be endowed, if she marries a man who is her equal?"

"Immediately, three talents of money; in the future, all that I possess."

"This gentleman of mine has long served me," Timon said. "Although he serves me, he is well born. As I said, he is a gentleman. To build his fortune I will strain a little because generosity is a duty among men. Give him your daughter. What you bestow to your daughter, I'll match and give to him. If the wealth of Lucilius and the wealth of your daughter were weighed in a pair of scales, they would weigh the same."

"Most noble lord, if you stake your honor to me that you will do this, she is his."

"Let's shake hands," Timon said. "I promise on my honor that I will do what I said I will do."

"Humbly I thank your lordship," Lucilius said. "May no property or fortune ever fall into my possession that I do not acknowledge as being due to you!"

Lucilius and the old Athenian man exited together.

The poet went to Timon, offered him a document, and said, "Please accept my labor, and long live your lordship!"

"I thank you," Timon said, accepting the document. "You shall hear from me soon. Don't go far away."

Timon then said to the painter as the poet went a short distance away, "What do you have there, my friend?"

"A piece of painting, which I ask your lordship to accept."

"Painting is welcome," Timon said, taking the painting. "The painted figure is almost the natural man who is free of artificiality. But since dishonor has dealings with man's nature, he is merely outward appearance: A man may appear to be other than he actually is. In contrast, these painted figures are exactly what they appear to be. I like your work, and you shall find I like it. Wait here in this hall until you hear further from me."

"May the gods preserve you!" the painter said.

"May you fare well, gentleman," Timon said to the painter. "Give me your hand. We must dine together."

Timon then turned to the jeweler and said, "Sir, your jewel has suffered under praise."

"What, my lord!" the jeweler said. "From underpraise? From dispraise?"

Timon explained what he had meant: "It has suffered from an excess of praise. If I should pay you for the jewel as it is praised, it would quite ruin me. The jewel is praised so highly that it must be very expensive."

"My lord, it is rated as those who sell would give," the jeweler said. "It is priced in accordance with what jewelers would normally pay for it; that is, it is priced at cost. But as you well know, things of like value that have different owners are prized differently by their owners — and other people will value the things differently according to who owns them. Two jewels may have the same objective value, but their owners may value them differently — and other people may value them differently according to who owns the jewels. Believe it, dear lord, when I say that you increase the jewel's value by wearing it."

"Well mocked," Timon said. "Well jested."

"No, my good lord," the merchant said. "He speaks the common tongue, which all men speak with him. Other men say the same thing that the jeweler did."

Seeing Apemantus coming toward him, Timon said, "Look and see who is coming here."

He said to the jeweler and the merchant, "Will you stay and be rebuked? You know that he will criticize all of us."

The jeweler replied, "We'll stay and endure his company, along with your lordship."

"He'll spare no one," the merchant said.

"Good day to you, gentle Apemantus!" Timon said.

"Until I become gentle, you will have to wait for me to wish you a good day; I will be gentle when you become your dog, and when these knaves become honest men. That will be never."

"Why do you call them knaves?" Timon asked. "You don't know them."

Hmm. Perhaps if Apemantus knew these men, he would be justified in calling them knaves.

"Aren't they Athenians?" Apemantus asked.

"Yes."

"Then I don't repent my calling them knaves," Apemantus said. "All Athenians are knaves."

The jeweler asked, "Do you know me, Apemantus?"

"You know I do. I called you by your name — knave."

"You are proud, Apemantus," Timon said.

Timon meant that Apemantus was arrogant and presumptuous, but Apemantus twisted the meaning of "proud."

"I am proud of nothing so much as that I am not like Timon."

Apemantus turned as if he were moving away, and Timon asked, "Where are you going?"

"To knock out an honest Athenian's brains."

"Murder is a crime. That's a deed you shall die for," Timon said.

"You are right," Apemantus said, "if doing nothing results in being put to death by the law."

In other words, no honest Athenian existed, and so Apemantus would knock out no honest Athenian's brains.

"How do you like this picture, Apemantus?" Timon asked, holding up the painting.

"I like it best for the innocence," Apemantus said.

The figure in the painting, not being a living being, could do no evil.

"Didn't the artist who painted it do a good job?"

"The man who made the painter — the painter's father — did a better job, and yet the painter's but a filthy piece of work."

"You're a dog," the painter said.

Apemantus was a Cynic philosopher who rejected materialism. The word "Cynic" was related to the Greek word for "doglike."

"Your mother's of my generation and breed," Apemantus said. "What is she, if I am a dog?"

He was calling the painter's mother a bitch.

"Will you dine with me, Apemantus?" Timon asked.

"No," Apemantus replied. "I don't eat lords."

He did not consume lords by eating their food and so consuming their wealth.

"If you did eat lords, you would anger the ladies," Timon said.

"Oh, they eat lords," Apemantus said. "That's how they come to have great big bellies."

By consuming the lords' food, the ladies grew great big bellies. By sexually consuming the lords, the ladies got pregnant.

"That's a lascivious apprehension," Timon said.

"Since that is how you apprehend — interpret — my words, take the apprehension for your labor."

"How do you like this jewel, Apemantus?" Timon asked, displaying it.

"Not so well as plain-dealing, which will not cost a man even a coin that is worth less than a penny."

Apemantus was referring to this proverb: "Plain-dealing is a jewel, but he who engages in plain-dealing dies a beggar." "Plain-dealing" is "honest dealing" — not cheating in business transactions.

"What do you think it is worth?" Timon asked.

"It's not worth my thinking about it," Apemantus said.

He then said, "How are you now, poet?"

"How are you now, philosopher?" the poet asked.

"You lie," Apemantus said.

"Aren't you a philosopher?" the poet asked.

"Yes."

"Then I'm not lying."

"Aren't you a poet?"

"Yes."

"Then you lie," Apemantus said.

A proverb stated, "Travelers and poets have leave to lie."

Travelers brought back home fantastic tales of their adventures.

As early as Plato, poets have been criticized for lying. In *The Republic*, Plato's character Socrates criticized Homer for lying about the gods by making them figures of fun instead of majestic beings. For example, in Homer's *Iliad*, Hera outwits her husband, Zeus, by having sex with him so that he will fall asleep and the Greeks, whom Hera supports, can rally against the Trojans in a battle of the Trojan War.

Apemantus continued, "Look in your last work of poetry, where you have depicted Timon as a worthy fellow."

"That's not feigned," the poet said. "It's not a lie. Timon really is worthy."

"Yes, he is worthy of you," Apemantus said, "and to pay you for your labor: He who loves to be flattered is worthy of the flatterer. Heavens, if I were a lord!"

"What would you do then, Apemantus?" Timon asked.

"I would do what I — Apemantus — do now; I would hate a lord with all my heart."

"What! Would you hate yourself?"

"Yes."

"Why?"

"Because I had no angry wit to be a lord," Apemantus said. "Because to be a lord I had no angry wit."

In order for Apemantus to be a lord, he would have to give up being a Cynic philosopher because Cynic philosophers rejected materialism and high social rank. Apemantus would have to give up the angry wit of a Cynic philosopher if he became a lord.

Apemantus also meant that if he became a lord, he would be a poor lord because he lacked the angry wit necessary to be a lord. Yes, he possessed the angry wit he needed to be a Cynic philosopher, but he lacked the angry wit he would need to be a lord. As a Cynic philosopher, he could direct his anger toward people whose behavior he disliked, but as a lord, he would have to behave in a way that he disliked and that would make him angry at himself for being a phony. Apemantus enjoyed mocking others; he had no desire to seriously mock himself or to do anything that would result in him mocking himself.

Apemantus would be intelligent either as a Cynic philosopher or as a lord. As a Cynic philosopher, he was intelligent enough to realize the foolishness of other people. As a lord, he would still be intelligent, and he would realize how foolish he — a lord — was. Most of the lords he knew were flatterers and hypocrites. Timon was a lord, but Apemantus regarded him as a fool for being deceived in the belief that he had true friends.

Apemantus then asked, "Aren't you a merchant?"

"Yes, I am, Apemantus," the merchant replied.

"May business ruin you, if the gods will not!"

"If business ruins me, then the gods ruin me," the merchant replied.

"Business is your god, and may your god ruin you!" Apemantus said.

A trumpet sounded, and a messenger entered the hall.

"Whose trumpet is that?" Timon asked.

The messenger replied, "It is the trumpet of Alcibiades, and some twenty horsemen, all in the same company."

Timon said to some attendants, "Please, welcome them; guide them here to us."

The attendants left to carry out their orders. The messenger went with them.

Timon said to Apemantus, "You must dine with me."

He said to the painter, "Don't go until I have thanked you. When dinner's done, show me this piece."

He then said to all who were present, "I am happy and joyful to see all of you here."

Alcibiades and others entered the hall.

Timon said, "Most welcome, sir!"

Much bowing took place.

Apemantus said, "Well, look at that! May your aches shrivel and wither your supple joints! That there should be little love among these sweet knaves, and yet there is all this courtesy! The strain of man's bred out into baboon and monkey. Men have degenerated and become baboons and monkeys."

Alcibiades said to Timon, "Sir, you have satisfied my longing to see you, and I feed most hungrily on your sight."

"You are very welcome, sir!" Timon said. "Before we part, we'll spend abundant time sharing various pleasures. If you please, let us go inside."

Everyone exited except for Apemantus.

Two lords arrived.

The first lord asked, "What time of day is it, Apemantus?"

"It is time to be honest."

"It is always that time," the first lord said.

"Then the more accursed are you, who always neglect it," Apemantus said.

"Are you going to Lord Timon's feast?" the second lord asked.

"Yes, to see food fill knaves and wine heat fools."

"Fare you well, fare you well," the second lord said.

"You are a fool to bid me farewell twice," Apemantus said.

"Why, Apemantus?" the second lord asked.

"You should have kept one farewell to yourself, for I mean to give you none."

"Go hang yourself!" the first lord said.

"No, I will do nothing at your bidding," Apemantus said. "Make your requests to your friend."

"Go away, quarrelsome dog, or I'll kick you away from here!" the second lord said.

"I will flee, like a dog, the heels of the ass," Apemantus said.

A dog will flee to avoid being kicked by the hooves of an angry donkey or ass.

Apemantus exited.

The first lord said, "Apemantus is opposed to humanity. Come, shall we go in, and taste Lord Timon's bounty? He outstrips and surpasses the very heart and soul of kindness."

"Timon pours his bounty out," the second lord said. "Plutus, the god of gold, is his steward. Timon receives no gifts that he does not repay sevenfold above the value of the gift. Every gift to Timon breeds the giver a return exceeding all the usual practice of repayment. Timon repays the gifts with much more than the usual rate of interest given for a loan."

"Timon carries the noblest mind that ever governed man."

"Long may he live with his fortunes!" the second lord said. "Shall we go in?"
"I'll keep you company," the first lord said.
They went in.

— 1.2 —

In a banqueting room in Timon's house, musicians were playing music and servants were carrying in great amounts of food. Present were Timon, Alcibiades, lords, Senators, and Ventidius, whose debt of five talents Timon had paid so that he could be released from prison. Apemantus walked into the room, looking unhappy as usual. Everyone except Apemantus was wearing fine clothing.

Ventidius said, "Most honored Timon, it has pleased the gods to remember my father's age, and call him to the long peace that is death. He is gone, he died well, and he has left me rich. So then, as in grateful virtue I am bound to your generous heart, I return to you those talents, doubled with thanks and respect, from whose help I derived liberty."

"Oh, by no means, honest Ventidius, will I accept your money," Timon said. "You misunderstand my friendship for you. I gave the money to you freely and forever, and no one can truly say that he gives, if he receives. Even if our betters play at that game — receiving back what they have given — we must not dare to imitate them; the faults of the rich are fair."

The "betters" were rich money-lending usurers, who received interest on their loans. The Senators of Athens did this.

A proverb stated, "The rich have no faults." In other words, behavior that would be considered a fault if done by a poor person is not considered a fault when done by a rich person.

"What a noble spirit you have!" Ventidius said.

The lords present stood to show respect to Timon.

Timon said, "No, my lords, ceremoniousness was devised at first to set a glossy but deceptive appearance on faint deeds, hollow welcomes, and goodness, generosity, and kindness that are quickly taken back — false goodness that is regretted even before it is shown. But where there is true friendship, ceremoniousness is not needed.

"Please, sit. More welcome are you to my fortunes than my fortunes are to me. I value you more than I value my vast wealth."

They sat.

The first lord said, "My lord, we always have confessed it."

He may have meant that the lords always have confessed to being friends with Timon, but a cynical person — such as Apemantus — could think that he meant that the lords always have confessed to being very welcome to Timon's vast wealth.

Apemantus said loudly, "Ho, ho, confessed it! Hanged it, have you not?"

He was alluding to this proverb: Confess (your crimes) and be hanged. However, meat was hung and dry aged to make it more flavorful, and the lords confessed their friendship to Timon and were rewarded with flavorful meat that had been hung.

"Oh, Apemantus, you are welcome," Timon said.

"No, you shall not make me welcome," Apemantus said. "I have come to have you throw me out of doors."

"Bah, you are a churl," Timon said. "You've got a disposition there that does not become a man. Your moodiness is much to blame for causing you to engage in inappropriate behavior."

Timon then said, "They say, my lords, '*Ira furor brevis est*' — Latin for 'Anger is a brief madness' — but yonder man is always angry. Go, let him have a table by himself, for he neither desires company, nor is he fit for it, indeed."

Servants brought out a table for Apemantus to sit at by himself.

"Let me stay at your peril, Timon," Apemantus said. "I come to observe; I give you warning on it."

By "observe," he meant both to see and to comment on what he saw.

"I take no heed of you," Timon said. "I won't pay attention to you. You are an Athenian, and therefore you are welcome. I myself have no power to make you be quiet, and so I hope that my food will make you silent."

"I scorn your food," Apemantus said. "It would choke me because it is for flatterers and I will never flatter you.

"Oh, you gods, what a number of men eat Timon, and he does not see them! It grieves me to see so many dip their food in one man's blood; and all the madness is that he encourages them to eat him up, too.

"I wonder that men dare trust themselves with men. I think that they should invite them without knives; that would be good for their food, and safer for their lives."

In this society, forks were mostly unknown and people brought their own knives to feasts. If his guests did not have knives, it would be good for Timon's food because the guests could not eat as much, and it would be safer for Timon because his guests could not murder him by slitting his throat with their knives.

Apemantus continued, "There's much example for it; the fellow who sits next to him now, divides and shares bread with him, and pledges his life to him while drinking a toast in a cup passed from person to person is the readiest man to kill him: It has been proven."

Judas Iscariot is one example whom Apemantus may have had in mind. Judas shared a meal with Jesus at the Last Supper before betraying him. At the Last Supper, Jesus invited his disciples to eat his body: "*And as they did eat, Jesus took the bread, and when he had blessed, he brake it, and gave it to the disciples, and said, Take, eat: this is my body*" (Matthew 26:26).

Apemantus continued, "If I were a huge — big in social status — man, I would be afraid to drink during meals at which guests were present lest they should spy where my windpipe makes its dangerous notes. Great men should drink while wearing armor to protect their throats."

Timon proposed a toast: "My lord, with heart and good spirits; and let the health — the toast — go round."

"Let it flow this way, my good lord," the second lord, who was eager to drink a toast, said.

"Flow this way!" Apemantus said. "He is a splendid fellow! He keeps his tides — his occasions and opportunities — well. Those healths will make you and your estate look ill, Timon."

He was referring to this proverb: "To drink healths is to drink sickness." Drinking too many toasts of alcohol will give one a hangover or do worse damage to one's health — and financial situation.

Apemantus lifted a cup of water and said, "Here's that which is too weak to be a sinner, honest water, which never left man in the mire. This cup of water and my food — edible roots — are equals; there's no difference between them. Both are healthy and inexpensive, and I thank the gods for both of them. People who attend feasts are too proud to give thanks to the gods."

Apemantus prayed:

"Immortal gods, I crave no pelf, aka possessions;

"I pray for no man but myself:

"Grant I may never prove so fond, aka foolish,

"To trust man on his oath or bond,

"Or a harlot, for her weeping,

"Or a dog, that seems to be sleeping,

"Or a jailer with my freedom,

"Or my friends, if I should need them.

"Amen."

He pulled an edible root from a pocket and said to himself, "So I fall to it. Rich men sin, and I eat roots. Much good dich your good heart, Apemantus!"

"Dich" was a dialectical word meaning "do" and "scour or clean." Apemantus was saying this: May my food keep me healthy and keep me consistent with my principles.

Timon said, "Captain Alcibiades, your heart's in the battlefield now."

"My heart is ever at your service, my lord," Alcibiades replied.

"You had rather be at a breakfast of enemies than a dinner of friends."

"As long as the enemies were newly bleeding, my lord, there's no food like them. I could wish my best friend at such a feast."

Apemantus said, "I wish that all those flatterers were your enemies, so that then you might kill them and bid me to eat them!"

The first lord said to Timon, "Might we but have that happiness, my lord, that you would once make use of our hearts, whereby we might express some part of our zealous friendship for you, we would think ourselves forever perfectly happy."

"Oh, no doubt, my good friends," Timon said, "but the gods themselves have provided that I shall have much help from you: How would you have become my friends otherwise? Why would you have that charitable and warmhearted title of friend from among so many thousands of other people if you did not chiefly belong to my heart? I have told more about you to myself than you can with modesty speak in your own behalf; and thus far I can vouch for your worthiness. I have narrated to myself your many merits.

"Oh, you gods, I think to myself, what need do we have for any friends, if we should never have need of them? Friends would be the most unnecessary creatures living, if we should never have any need to use them, and they would most resemble sweet-sounding musical instruments hung up in cases that keep their sounds to themselves.

"Why, I have often wished myself poorer, so that I might come nearer to you. We are born to do good deeds, and what better or more properly can we call our own than the riches of our friends?

"Oh, what a precious comfort it is, to have so many friends, like brothers, commanding one another's fortunes! Oh, joy, that seems to be finished because of the appearance of tears, which actually are happy, even before joy can be completely born!

"My eyes cannot keep from watering, I think. To forget the faults of my eyes, I drink to you."

Apemantus said, "You weep to make them drink, Timon."

Timon's weeping provided an occasion for all to drink, but all his guests' drinking and eating at his expense would soon cause Timon to weep.

The second lord said, "Joy had the like conception in our eyes, and at that instant like a babe it sprung up."

Apemantus chuckled and said, "I laugh to think that babe a bastard."

A bastard is falsely conceived, and the tears in the eyes of the lords were falsely conceived. They were the tears of hypocrisy and flattery, not the tears of shared friendship.

"I promise you, my lord, you moved me much," the third lord said.

"Much!" Apemantus said. "Much I believe that!"

A trumpet sounded.

"What is the meaning of that trumpet?" Timon asked.

A servant entered, and Timon asked him, "What is it?"

"If it pleases you, my lord, certain ladies greatly want to be admitted here," the servant replied.

"Ladies!" Timon said. "What do they want?"

"There comes with them a forerunner, my lord, who has the job of telling you what they want," the servant said.

"All right, let them be admitted here."

A boy dressed as Cupid, the young son of Venus, goddess of sexual passion, entered the dining hall.

The Cupid said, "Hail to you, worthy Timon, and to all who taste his bounty and enjoy his acts of kindness! The five best senses acknowledge you as their patron, and they come freely to greet your generous warm-heartedness.

There, taste, touch, and smell, all pleased from your table rise; the ladies who come now come only to feast your eyes."

"They're all welcome," Timon said. "Let them kindly be admitted. Musicians, make them welcome!"

The Cupid exited to get the ladies.

"You see, my lord, how amply you're beloved," the first lord said.

Music began to play. Cupid returned with several ladies costumed as Amazons, a tribe of warrior women. They had lutes in their hands, and they danced as they played the lutes.

"Hey, what a sweep of vanity and foolishness comes this way!" Apemantus said. "They dance! They are madwomen. A similar madness — vanity — is the glory of this life. Just look at all this fancy food when all that anyone needs is a little oil and some edible roots. We make ourselves fools to entertain ourselves, and we expend our flatteries to drink down those men upon whose old age we vomit the drink up again with poisonous spite and envy. Society flatters men when they are in the prime earning years of their lives, and then society rejects them when they are old.

"Who lives who is not slandered or slanders? Who dies and goes to their grave who has not suffered from at least one kick that their friends gave them?

"I would fear that those who dance before me now will one day stomp on me. Before this it has been done; men shut their doors against a setting sun."

Sun worshippers say prayers to the *rising* morning Sun, which they worship and adore.

Timon sat down as the lords stood up to show their loves for and to dance with the Amazons, who had finished their ceremonious dancing.

Once the dance of the lords and the Amazons was over, Timon said, "You have brought to our entertainment much gracefulness, fair ladies. You have set a fair fashion on our entertainment, which before you arrived was not half as beautiful and gracious as you have made it. You have added worth and luster to our entertainment, and you have entertained me at my own feast. I thank you for it."

"My lord, you take us even at the best," the first lady said. "You rate our performance as highly as it can be rated."

"It is good to sexually take them at their best," Apemantus said, "for to sexually take them at their worst is filthy, and would not be worth the taking, I fear. When ladies are at their worst, their vaginas are diseased."

"Ladies, a little banquet of fruits, desserts, and wine is waiting for you," Timon said. "Please go and enjoy yourselves."

"We will, most thankfully, my lord," the ladies said.

The Cupid and the ladies exited.

Timon called for his steward: "Flavius."

A steward is in charge of the household; his job includes paying bills and managing household finances.

Flavius said, "My lord?"

"Bring to me here the little casket."

Leaving to get the little casket, which contained jewels, some of which Timon intended to give away, Flavius said to himself, "Yet more jewels! There's no speaking to him when he is in the giving mood, I can't cross his wishes, or else I would tell him — well, truly I should tell him that when he has spent everything, he'll want to be crossed then, if he could."

Timon was so generous that he was going bankrupt and did not realize it. When he had spent everything, including all he could borrow, he would want his debts crossed off, as they would be if they had been paid. He would also want his palms crossed with silver — for example, with silver coins that had been stamped with the image of a cross.

Flavius continued, "It is a pity that bounty — generosity — had not eyes behind, in the back of the head, so that a man might never be made wretched because of his generous mind."

Flavius exited.

The first lord asked, "Where are our servants?"

A servant replied, "Here we are, my lord, standing in readiness to serve you."

The second lord said, "Bring our horses!"

Flavius returned with the little casket of jewels.

Timon said, "Oh, my friends, I have a few words to say to you."

He said to the first lord, "Look, my good lord, I must ask you to much honor me by accepting this jewel and wearing it and making it more valuable by your wearing it, my kind lord."

The first lord said, "I have already received so many of your gifts —"

The other lords said, "So have we all."

A servant entered and said to Timon, "My lord, certain nobles of the Senate have just now alighted from their horses, and are coming to visit you."

"They are very welcome," Timon said.

Flavius said to Timon, "I beg your honor, let me say a few words to you that seriously concern you."

"Seriously concern me! Why then, another time I'll hear you. Right now, let's have provided what is needed to entertain the new visitors."

Flavius murmured to himself, "I scarcely know how to do that."

A second servant entered the dining hall and said, "May it please your honor, Lord Lucius, out of his free and generous love, has presented to you four milk-white horses, with silver trappings."

"I shall accept them fairly," Timon said. "Let the presents be worthily dealt with."

A third servant arrived, and Timon asked, "What is it? What's the news you have for me?"

"If it pleases you, my lord, that honorable gentleman, Lord Lucullus, entreats your company tomorrow to hunt with him, and he has sent your honor two pairs of greyhounds."

"I'll hunt with him," Timon said, "and let the greyhounds be received, but not without a fair reward."

Timon meant to pay for the greyhounds, although they were a gift.

"What will this come to?" Flavius said to himself. "Timon commands us to provide and to give away great gifts, and all out of an empty coffer. Nor will he let me tell him his net worth, which is negative, or allow me to show him what a beggar his heart is because it has no power to make his wishes good. His promises fly so beyond his estate and possessions that what he speaks is all in debt; he owes for every word. He is so kind that he now pays interest on the loans he has taken out so that he can be generous. His land's mortgaged and on the books of those to whom he gives gifts.

"Well, I wish that I were gently put out of my job as his steward before I am forced out! Happier is he who has no friends to feed than friends who even enemies exceed. His friends cost him more than enemies would. I bleed inwardly for my lord."

Flavius exited.

Timon said to the lords, his guests, "You do yourselves much wrong by lessening too much your own merits: You are too critical of yourselves."

He gave a jewel to the second lord and said, "Here, my lord, is a small token of our friendship for each other."

"With more than common thanks, I will accept it," the second lord said.

The third lord said about Timon, "Oh, he's the very soul of bounty!"

Hearing the third lord, Timon said, "And now I remember, my lord, you said good words of praise the other day about a bay stallion I rode on: It is yours, because you liked it."

"Oh, I beg that you pardon me, my lord, in that," the third lord said.

Perhaps the third lord meant that he wanted to be forgiven for having seemed to beg for the stallion by praising it. A cynical man such as Apemantus would think that the third lord was putting on an act now, and that the third lord really had praised the stallion in the hope that Timon would give it to him.

"You may believe my words, my lord," Timon said, "when I say that I know no man can justly affect — praise — nothing but what he really does like. I weigh my friends' affection with my own; I regard as equally important my friends' wishes and my own, to tell you the truth."

He then said to the lords, "I'll call on you."

Timon meant that he would visit them, but soon he would call on the lords for loans.

"No one is as welcome as you," the lords said.

"I take all of your many visits to me so kindly to heart that it is not enough for me to give you what I give," Timon said. "I think that I could give kingdoms to my friends, and never be weary of giving."

He then said, "Alcibiades, you are a soldier, and therefore you are seldom rich; what I give to you comes in charity to you because all your living is among the dead, and all the lands you have lie in a pitched field."

"Yes, the pitched field is defiled land, my lord," Alcibiades replied.

He was punning. In the Apocrypha, Ecclesiasticus 13:1 states, "*He that touchest pitch shall be defiled with it.*" Pitch is a tar-like substance, and a pitched field is a battlefield is which lines, aka files, of soldiers are ready to engage in battle.

The first lord began to speak, "We are so virtuously bound —"

Timon interrupted, "— and so am I to all of you."

The second lord began to speak, "So infinitely bound in affection —"

Timon again interrupted, "— and so am I to all of you."

He then ordered, "Lights, more lights!"

The first lord said, "May the best of happiness, honor, and fortunes always be with you, Lord Timon!"

Timon said, "— so that he can keep them ready for his friends."

Everyone left the great dining hall except for Apemantus and Timon.

"What a noisy disturbance is here!" Apemantus said. "What a serving of bows and jutting-out of butts! I doubt whether their legs are worth the sums that are given for them. How much money they make for their bowing! Friendship is full of dregs and impurities; I think that false hearts should never have sound legs. False friends should not be healthy enough to bow. Thus honest fools lay out their wealth on courtesies. Timon gives away many valuables to those who bow to him."

Timon said, "Now, Apemantus, if you were not sullen, I would be good to you. I would be generous to you."

"No, I'll accept nothing," Apemantus replied, "for if I should be bribed, too, there would be no one left to rail upon and criticize you, and then you would sin all the faster. You have given away so much for so long, Timon, that I am afraid that you will have nothing to give away except IOUs shortly. What is the need for these feasts, pompous activities, and vainglorious events?"

"Whenever you begin to rail against society, I am sworn not to give any notice to you," Timon said. "Farewell, and come back again with better music — with noncritical words."

Timon exited.

Apemantus said to himself, "So be it. You will not hear me now; you shall not hear me later. I'll lock your Heaven away from you by not giving you the advice that would keep you happy. Oh, that men's ears should be deaf to good advice, but not to flattery!"

CHAPTER 2

— 2.1 —

Examining some financial papers in his house, a Senator said to himself about Timon, "... and lately, five thousand. To Varro and to Isidore he owes nine thousand; besides my former sum, which makes it five and twenty. Still in motion of raging waste? His wastefulness with money is like a raging flood. It cannot hold; it will not hold. He cannot continue like this and be solvent. If I want gold, all I need to do is to steal a beggar's dog, and give it to Timon — why, the dog coins gold for me when Timon rewards me with a gift."

Dogs were sometimes trained to lead blind beggars.

The Senator continued, "If I want to sell my horse, and buy twenty more horses better than it, why, all I need to do is to give my horse to Timon — ask nothing for it, but just give it to him — and it immediately foals for me strong, healthy horses. No porter is at his gate to keep away unwelcome visitors; instead, he has a porter who smiles and always invites inside all who pass by. This state of affairs cannot hold, it cannot continue, no rational person can examine Timon's financial affairs and think that Timon's estate is safe. If we were to sound the depth of his wealth, we would find it growing shallower and shallower — no ship could safely sail on it. The only thing growing deeper is his debts."

The Senator called a servant, "Caphis, ho! Caphis, I say!"

Caphis entered the room and said, "Here I am, sir; what is your pleasure? What do you want me to do?"

"Put on your cloak, and hasten to Lord Timon. Importune him for my money that he owes me; don't be put off with an offhand denial, and don't then be silenced when he says, 'Commend me to your master,' and takes off his cap and plays with it in his right hand, like this."

The Senator demonstrated what he meant, and then he continued, "Instead, tell him that my financial needs cry to me, and I must meet my need with my own money; the days and times that he ought to have repaid his debt to me are past and my reliance on his broken promises to repay me has hurt my credit. I love and honor him, but I must not break my back to heal his finger;

immediate and pressing are my needs, and my relief must not be tossed and returned to me in words like a ball in tennis, but it must find a supply of money immediately.

"Get you gone. Put a very pressing, insistent look on your face, a visage of demand, because I am afraid that when every borrowed feather is returned and is stuck in the wing of the bird to whom the feather belongs, Lord Timon will be left a naked gull, although now he flashes like the remarkable mythological bird we call the phoenix. Get you gone."

"I go, sir," Caphis said.

"Take the bonds along with you, and clearly mark the due dates of the loans."

"I will, sir."

"Go."

Just outside Timon's house, Flavius, holding many past-due bills in his hands, talked to himself.

"No care, no stop! Timon is so senseless of expense that he will neither learn how to maintain the income to pay his expenses, nor cease his flow of riotous extravagance. He takes no account of how valuable things go away from him, nor does he assume any care about what is needed for him to continue his extravagant spending and giving of gifts. Never has a mind been so foolish as to be so kind. What shall be done? He will not listen to me until he feels the result of his extravagance. I must be blunt with him once he returns from hunting."

He saw Caphis and the servants of Isidore and of Varro coming and said, "Damn! Damn! Damn! Damn!"

Caphis said, "Good afternoon, Varro's servant. Have you come for money?"

Varro's servant replied, "Isn't that your business here, too?"

"Yes, it is," Caphis said, "and is it yours, too, Isidore's servant?"

Isidore's servant replied, "It is."

"I wish that we were all paid!" Caphis said.

"I am afraid that that won't happen," Varro's servant said.

"Here comes lord Timon," Caphis said.

Returning from their hunt, Timon, Alcibiades, some lords, and others arrived.

Timon said, "As soon as we've eaten dinner, we'll go out again, my Alcibiades."

Seeing the people waiting for him, he said, "Do you have business with me? What do you want?"

Caphis said, "My lord, here is a note of certain dues. You owe my master money."

"Dues! From where are you?" Timon asked. His land holdings were vast and stretched all the way to Lacedaemon, where the city of Sparta was located, and he did not recognize Caphis.

"I am from Athens, my lord," Caphis replied.

"Go and see Flavius, my steward," Timon said.

"Please, your lordship, he has put me off from day to day all this month. My master is forced by important business to call for repayment of his own money, and he humbly requests that you, in accordance with your other noble qualities, will give to him what is rightfully his."

Timon said, "My honest friend, please return to me tomorrow morning."

"No, my good lord —" Caphis said forcefully.

"Be calm, good friend," Timon said. "Restrain yourself."

Varro's servant said, "I am one of Varro's servants, my good lord —"

Isidore's servant said, "I come from Isidore; he humbly asks for your speedy payment."

Caphis said, "If you knew, my lord, my master's need for money —"

Varro's servant said, "The note was due on forfeiture, my lord, six weeks ago — and more."

Timon had borrowed money by pledging security for it. All of his land was mortgaged, and the land would be forfeited if he could not repay his debts.

Isidore's servant said, "Your steward puts me off, my lord, and so I am sent expressly to your lordship to ask for repayment of the loan."

"Give me room to breathe," Timon said to the three servants who were crowding around him.

He then said to Alcibiades and the other lords with whom he had been hunting, "Please, my good lords, go inside. I'll follow and be with you quickly."

Alcibiades and the other lords went inside.

Seeing Flavius, Timon said, "Come here. Please tell me what is wrong with the world that I thus encounter clamorous demands about broken bonds and I hear about the failure to pay long-since-due debts, which are things that are contrary to and hurt my reputation?"

Flavius said to the three servants asking Timon for money, "If you please, gentlemen, the time is unsuitable for this business. Stop importuning Timon for money until after dinner so that I may make his lordship understand why you are not paid."

"Do that, my friends," Timon said to the three servants.

He then said to Flavius, "See that they are well entertained."

He went inside.

Flavius said to the three servants, "Please, come with me."

He went inside.

Apemantus and a Fool, whose job was to entertain his boss — in this case, a woman — and make her laugh, walked nearby. Seeing Apemantus and the Fool, the three servants stayed outside rather than immediately go inside Timon's house.

Caphis said, "Wait, wait. Here comes the Fool with Apemantus. Let's have some fun with them."

Varro's servant said, "Hang Apemantus — he'll abuse us with words."

Isidore's servant said, "A plague upon him, the dog!"

Varro's servant asked, "How are you doing, Fool?"

Apemantus asked, "Are you talking to your shadow?"

"I am not speaking to you," Varro's servant said.

"No, you are speaking to yourself," Apemantus said.

He then said to the Fool, "Let's go."

Isidore's servant said to Varro's servant, "There's the fool hanging on your back already."

He meant that the name of fool had been affixed to the back of Varro's servant. It was like Varro's servant was wearing the distinctive clothing of a professional Fool. He also meant that Varro's servant was being ridden — criticized — by a fool.

Apemantus said to Isidore's servant, "No, you are standing alone and by yourself — you are not on him yet."

Apemantus meant by this kind of riding homosexual riding.

"Where's the fool now?" Caphis asked Isidore's servant. "Who is really the fool?"

Sparing none of the three servants, Apemantus said to Caphis, "The fool is he who last asked the question 'Who is the fool?'"

He then said about the three servants, "Poor rogues, and usurers' men! You are bawds between gold and want!"

A want can be a need; people can need or want money and people can need or want sex.

Usurers were people who lent money at interest, something that many people in this society felt that the god of Christians prohibited. Usurers were often compared to bawds, aka pimps, because both trafficked in money when money ought not to be involved. Money ought not to be lent at interest, and money ought not to be exchanged for sex.

"What are we, Apemantus?" the three servants asked.

"You are asses."

"Why?"

"Because you ask me what you are, and you do not know yourselves," Apemantus said.

He then said, "Speak to them, Fool."

"How are you, gentlemen?" the Fool asked.

"Thank you for asking, good Fool," the servants said. "How is your mistress?"

"Mistress" simply meant "female boss."

"She's just now setting water on a fire to heat up and scald such chickens as you are," the Fool said.

Chickens were scalded in boiling water to remove their feathers. Another kind of chicken — young fools — sat in hot water as a treatment for venereal disease.

The Fool added, "I wish that we could see you at Corinth!"

Corinth was a Greek port city famous for its brothels. The red-light district of Athens was referred to in slang as Corinth.

"Good!" Apemantus said to the Fool. "Many thanks!"

He was thanking the Fool for speaking to and insulting the servants.

"Look," the Fool said. "Here comes my mistress' page."

The page, a young servant, walked over and said to the Fool, "Why, what's going on, Captain? What are you doing in this wise company?"

The page then asked, "How are you, Apemantus?"

"I wish that I had a rod in my mouth, so that I could answer you profitably."

Apemantus was referring to these 1599 Geneva Bible verses:

Proverbs 22:15

Foolishness is bound in the heart of a child: but the rod of correction shall drive it away from him.

Proverbs 23:13-14:

13 Withhold not correction from the child: if thou smite him with the rod, he shall not die.

14 Thou shalt smite him with the rod, and shalt deliver his soul from hell.

Proverbs 26:3:

Unto the horse belongeth a whip, to the ass a bridle, and a rod to the fool's back.

The page said, "Please, Apemantus, read me the addresses on these letters. I don't know which is which."

Apemantus asked, "Can't you read?"

"No."

"Little learning will die then on the day you are hanged," Apemantus said.

He looked at the letters and said, "This letter is addressed to Lord Timon; this one is addressed to Alcibiades. Go; you were born a bastard, and you'll die a bawd."

The page replied, "You were whelped as a dog, and you shall famish and die of starvation and so die a dog's death. Don't answer me, for I am gone."

The page exited.

Taking the word "gone" to mean "damned," Apemantus said to the page's back, "Even so you are outrunning grace."

He meant that his words of criticism could keep the page out of Hell if the page were to learn from the criticism.

Apemantus then said, "Fool, I will go with you to Lord Timon's."

"Will you leave me there?" the Fool asked.

"If Timon stays at home," Apemantus said, meaning that as long as Timon was at home, a fool was in his home.

Apemantus asked the three servants, "Do you three serve three usurers?"

"Yes; we wish that they served us!"

"So do I — I wish that they served you as good a trick as ever a hangman served a thief," Apemantus said.

"Are you three usurers' men?" the Fool asked.

"Yes, Fool."

"I think no usurer lacks a fool to serve as his servant," the Fool said. "My mistress is a usurer, in her own way, which is that of a bawd, and I am her Fool. When men come to borrow from your masters, they approach sadly, and go away merrily; but they enter my mistress' house merrily, and go away sadly. Why is this?"

Men with light pockets went to the usurer; leaving the usurer, they had heavy pockets. Men with heavy pockets went to the bawd; leaving the bawd, they had light pockets.

Varro's servant said, "I can give you a reason."

"Do it then," Apemantus said, "so that we may know that you are a whoremaster and a knave, which notwithstanding, you shall be no less esteemed than you are now."

Being the servant of a usurer had the same status as being the servant of a bawd.

"What is a whoremaster, Fool?" Varro's servant asked. He knew what a whoremaster was — a person who used the services of whores — but he wanted to hear the Fool make a joke.

"A whoremaster is a fool who wears good clothes, and he is something like you," the Fool said. "The whoremaster is a spirit. Sometime he looks like a lord; sometimes he looks like a lawyer; sometimes he looks like a philosopher, with two stones more than his artificial one."

The artificial stone was the philosopher's stone, which alchemists believed could turn base metal into gold. The philosopher's two natural stones were his testicles.

The Fool continued, "The whoremaster very often looks like a knight; and, generally, the whoremaster takes on the appearance of all shapes that man goes up and down in from fourscore to thirteen."

"Up and down" is a motion made in sex; it is also what happens to a penis when its owner is between eighty and thirteen years old.

Varro's servant said, "You are not altogether a fool."

Many Fools are wise.

The Fool replied, "Nor are you altogether a wise man. As much foolery as I have, just as much wit you lack."

Apemantus, who much appreciated the joke, said, "That answer might have come from me: Apemantus."

The three servants said, "Step aside, step aside. Here comes Lord Timon."

Timon and Flavius approached the group of men.

Apemantus said, "Come with me, Fool, come."

The Fool replied, "I do not always follow lover, elder brother, and woman; sometimes I follow the philosopher."

According to various proverbs, lovers, elder brothers, and women were all thought to be foolish:

It is impossible to love and be wise.
The younger brother has the more wit.
"Because" is a woman's reason.

Apemantus and the Fool exited.

Flavius said to the three servants, "Please, walk a little distance away so that I can talk with Timon privately. I'll speak with you soon."

The servants exited.

"You make me marvel," Timon said. "Why before this time did you not fully lay the state of my financial affairs before me, so that I might have estimated my expenses and my means of paying them? I could have lessened my expenses to fit my income."

"You would not hear me out," Flavius replied. "Many times when you were at leisure I proposed to explain to you the state of your financial affairs."

"Bah!" Timon said. "Perhaps you proposed to do that at a few opportune times, but my indisposition put you off, and my indisposition at those times served as your excuse not to bring up the matter again."

"Oh, my good lord, many times I brought in my accounts to you and laid them before you; you would throw them off the table, and say that you found me to be honest and so you had no need to examine the accounts. When, for some trifling present, you have ordered me to give the giver a much larger gift, I have shaken my head and wept. Yes, in opposition to the good manners a servant owes a master, I have requested that you hold your hand more closed — you were too open-handed with your wealth and possessions. Not seldom have I endured not-slight rebukes, when I have informed you of the ebb of your estate and your great flow of debts. My loved lord, although you hear me now, too late — yet now's a time, for late is better than never — your possessions even rated at their greatest possible value won't pay even half of your present debts."

"Let all of my land be sold," Timon said.

"All of your land is mortgaged," Flavius replied. "Some of it has been forfeited because of nonpayment of debts and is gone, and what remains will hardly stop the mouths of creditors calling for present dues. The future comes apace. What shall we do in the meantime? And what can we do in the future?"

"To Lacedaemon did my land extend," Timon said.

"Oh, my good lord, the world is but a word. Were the world all yours to give away in a breath, how quickly would it be gone!"

"You are telling me the truth," Timon said.

"If you suspect my husbandry of falsehood, call me before the most exacting auditors and put me on trial. So the gods bless me, I swear that when all our kitchens, butteries, and serving rooms have been oppressed with riotous feeders, when our wine cellars have wept with drunken spills of wine, when every room has blazed with lights and drunken asses have brayed with minstrel songs, I have retired to a wine cellar by a wasteful, running spigot, and my eyes have flown with tears to add to the spillage."

"Please, no more." Timon was referring both to Flavius' flow of words and current flow of tears.

"Heavens, I have said, the bounty and generosity of this lord! How many prodigal bites of food have slaves and peasants this night swallowed! Who is not Timon's friend? What heart, head, sword, force, fellowship, but is Lord Timon's? Great Timon, noble, worthy, royal Timon!

"Ah, when the means are gone that buy this praise, the breath is gone whereof this praise is made. Feast-won, fast-lost. The 'friends' who are won by feasts are quickly lost when the 'friends' are forced to fast. When one cloud of winter showers appears, these flies — parasites — seek shelter elsewhere."

"Come, sermon me no further," Timon said. "No villainous act of bounty and generosity yet has passed my heart. I have given unwisely, but not ignobly. Why do you weep? Can you lack knowledge? Can you actually think I shall lack friends? Set your heart free from worry. If I would broach the vessels of my love, and test the contents of my friends' hearts by borrowing from them, I would be able to borrow from men — my friends — and use their fortunes as frankly as I can bid you to speak. They would help me the way that you serve me."

"Broach the vessels of my love" meant to tap his friends the way that a barrel of wine is tapped. Timon expected that his friends would be full of generosity, and not just full of his wine.

"May assurance bless your thoughts!" Flavius said. "May what you say be true!"

"And, in a way, these needs of mine can be regarded as blessings; for by these I will test my friends. You shall perceive how you are mistaken about my fortunes; I am wealthy in my friends."

He called, "Inside there! Flaminius! Servilius!"

Flaminius, Servilius, and other servants appeared.

"My lord?" they said.

"I will dispatch you separately to some of my friends," Timon said.

Pointing to various servants, he said, "Servilius, you go to Lord Lucius. Flaminius, you go to Lord Lucullus; I hunted with his honor today."

He ordered a third servant, "You go to Sempronius."

He then said to the servants, "Commend me to their friendships, and say that I am proud that my situation has made this an opportune time to ask them to supply me with money. Let the request be for fifty talents."

Flaminius said, "We will do what you have said, my lord."

Flavius was skeptical that Timon would get money. He thought, *Lord Lucius and Lord Lucullus? Hmm!*

Timon said to Flavius, "Go you, sir, to the Senators — because of what I have done to ensure the state's best health, I deserve for them to hear this request — ask them to send immediately a thousand talents to me."

Flavius replied, "I have been bold — because I knew that it was the best way to get money to pay the most creditors — to go to them and use the seal of your signet ring and your name to ask them for money, but they shook their heads, and I returned here no richer."

"Is it true?" Timon asked. "Can it be true?"

"They answered, in a joint and corporate and united voice, that now they are at a low ebb, lack treasure, cannot do what they want to do, are sorry ... you are honorable ... but yet they could have wished ... they know not ... something has been amiss ... a noble nature may suffer a mishap ... wish that all were well ... it is a pity — and so, turning to other serious matters, after looks of distaste at this subject matter and after uttering these hard fragments of sentences, with certain half-courteous and cold nods they froze me into silence."

"You gods, reward them!" Timon said. "Please, man, look cheerful. These old fellows have their ingratitude in them through heredity and original sin. Because of their old age, their blood is caked, it is cold, it seldom flows. Because of a lack of kindly warmth, they are not kind. Human nature, as it grows again toward earth — old people become stooped — is made ready for the journey to the grave, for it becomes dull and heavy."

He ordered a servant, "Go to Ventidius."

He said to Flavius, "Please, don't be sad. You are true and honest; I am speaking ingenuously. No blame belongs to you."

He said to the servant, "Ventidius recently buried his father, by whose death he's stepped into a great estate. When he was poor, was imprisoned, and lacked friends, I cleared his debt by paying five talents. Greet him from me. Tell him to suppose some good necessity touches his friend, who craves to be remembered with those five talents. Ask him to return to me those five talents I paid to clear his debt and get him out of prison."

The servant exited.

He then said to Flavius, "Once you have those five talents, give it to these fellows to whom it is now due. Never say, or think, that Timon's fortunes among his friends can sink."

Flavius replied, "I wish I could not think it. That thought is bounty's foe."

If one thinks that one's friends are parasites, then one will not be generous to them.

Flavius continued, "Being free and generous himself, a generous person thinks all others so."

CHAPTER 3

— 3.1 —

Alone, Flaminius waited in a room in Lucullus' house.

A servant arrived and said to him, "I have told my lord about you; he is coming down to you."

"I thank you, sir."

Lucullus entered the room, and the servant said, "Here's my lord."

Seeing Flaminius, Lucullus said to himself, "One of Lord Timon's servants? He has a gift from Timon for me, I bet. Why, I should have expected this; I dreamt of a silver basin and pitcher last night."

He then said out loud, "Flaminius, honest Flaminius; you are very respectfully welcome, sir."

He ordered his servant, "Fill a glass for me with some wine."

The servant exited.

Lucullus asked, "And how is that honorable, complete, free-hearted gentleman of Athens, your very bountiful good lord and master, doing?"

"His health is good, sir," Flaminius said.

"I am very glad that his health is good, sir, and what do you there have under your cloak, excellent Flaminius?"

"Truly, I have nothing but an empty box, sir," Flaminius replied. "In my lord's behalf, I have come to entreat your honor to fill it with money. My master, Timon, having great and immediate need to borrow fifty talents, has sent to your lordship to furnish him with that money. Timon does not at all doubt that you will immediately provide him with your assistance."

"Hmm! Hmm! Hmm! Hmm!" Lucullus said. "'Not at all doubt,' he said? Alas, good lord! He would be a noble gentleman, if he would not keep so generous a house. Many a time and often I have dined with him, and told him not to be so generous, and then I have come again to eat supper with him, with the purpose of persuading him to spend less, and yet he would embrace no advice and take no warning from my coming. Every man has his fault, and generosity is his. I have told him about it, but I could never get him to stop being generous."

Lucullus' servant returned, carrying wine.

"If it pleases your lordship, here is the wine," the servant said.

"Flaminius, I have always known you to be wise. Here's to you."
Lucullus drank.

"Your lordship speaks what it pleases you to say," Flaminius replied.

Lucullus said to Flaminius, "I have observed that you always have a helpful and ready-and-willing spirit — to give you your due — and that you are a man who knows what belongs to reason. You can use the time well, if the time uses — treats — you well. You can take advantage of a good opportunity, and you have good qualities in you."

He then said to his servant, "You can leave now."

His servant exited.

"Come closer to me, honest Flaminius," Lucullus said. "Your lord's a bountiful gentleman, but you are wise and you know well enough, although you have come to me, that this is no time to lend money, especially upon bare friendship, without some security such as land that can be forfeited if the loan is not repaid in time. Here are three coins for you. Good boy, wink at me — close your eyes — and say that you did not see me. Fare you well."

"Is it possible that the world should change so much, and that we who are now alive have lived through such major change?" Flaminius said. "Fly, damned baseness, back to him who worships you!"

He threw the three coins back to Lucullus.

"Bah!" Lucullus said. "Now I see that you are a fool and fit for your master."
Lucullus exited.

"May those three coins add to the number that may scald you!" Flaminius said. "Let molten coins be your damnation. You are a disease of a friend, and not a true friend!"

Contrapasso is an Italian term for an appropriate punishment. Many people think that the punishments in Hell for sins are *contrapassos*, and so the punishment for greed could be being dipped in molten gold.

Flaminius continued, "Has friendship such a faint and milky heart that it turns sour and curdles in less than two nights? Oh, you gods, I feel my master's passion — his agony! This slave, up to this hour, has my lord's food inside him. Why should my master's food thrive and turn to nutriment, when my master's 'friend' is turned to poison? Oh, may only diseases be caused by my master's food that this 'friend' has eaten! And, when Lucullus is sick to death, let not that part of him that my lord paid for, have any power to expel sickness — instead, let it prolong his agony and lengthen the time it takes him to die!"

Lucius spoke with three strangers in a public place in Athens.

"Who, the Lord Timon?" Lucius said. "He is my very good friend, and he is an honorable gentleman."

"We know him to be no less," the first stranger said, "although we are but strangers to him. But I can tell you one thing, my lord, which I hear from common rumors. Lord Timon's happy hours are now done and past, and his estate shrinks from him. He is losing his wealth."

"Bah, no, do not believe it," Lucius said. "Timon cannot need money. He is extremely wealthy."

"Believe this, my lord," the second stranger said. "Not long ago, one of Timon's men was with Lord Lucullus to borrow so many talents — indeed, Timon's servant urgently requested the loan and showed how necessary the loan was, and yet was denied the loan."

The second stranger did not know the exact number of talents that Timon was attempting to borrow other than Timon wanted to borrow many talents, and so he used the phrase "so many talents."

"What!" Lucius said.

"I tell you that Timon was denied the loan, my lord," the second stranger said.

"What a strange case was that!" Lucius said. "Now, before the gods, I swear that I am ashamed to hear it. That honorable man was denied a loan! There was very little honor showed in the denial. As for my own part, I must confess that I have received some small kindnesses from Timon, such as money, gold and silver household utensils, jewels, and such-like trifles, although nothing compared to what Lucullus received from Timon, yet had Timon sent a servant by mistake to ask me for a loan, I would never have denied his occasion so many talents."

His words were ambiguous.

"Occasion" can mean 1) "need," and it can mean 2) "favorable set of circumstances":

1) "I would never have denied his need so many talents" meant that he would lend Timon the money Timon needed.

2) "I would never have denied his favorable set of circumstances so many talents" meant that he would lend Timon the money as long as Timon did not actually need the money (and so would be sure to repay it, most likely with a large amount of self-imposed interest).

"Deny" can mean 1) "refuse to give someone something," and it can mean 2) "refuse to admit the truth of something":

1) "I would never have denied [for] his need so many talents" meant that he would lend Timon the money Timon needed; he would not refuse to give Timon the money.

2) "I would never have denied his need [for] so many talents" or "I would never have denied so many talents [to be] his need" meant that he would acknowledge Timon's need for the money (but may or may not lend him the money); he would not refuse to admit the truth that Timon needed money.

Servilius arrived on the scene and said to himself, "I see, by good luck, yonder is the lord, Lucius, whom I have worked hard and sweated to find."

He said to Lucius, "My honored lord —"

Lucius wished to avoid Servilius, whom he recognized as having been sent to him by Timon, who was currently asking friends for loans of money, so he said, "Servilius! You are kindly met, sir. Fare you well. Commend me to your honorable and virtuous lord, my very exquisite friend."

He started to leave.

"May it please your honor, my lord has sent —" Servilius began.

"Ha!" Lucius said, thinking that the stranger was wrong and that Timon was still rich and still giving gifts. "What has he sent? I am so much endeared to that lord; he's always sending something to me. How shall I thank him, do you think? And what has he sent me now?"

"He has sent only his present need now, my lord," Servilius said, handing Lucius a note from Timon. "He is requesting your lordship to supply so many talents for his immediate use."

"I know his lordship is just joking with me," Lucius said. "He cannot need fifty — or even five hundred — talents."

Lucius was trying to make the point that Timon, who was asking to borrow fifty talents, was so rich that fifty — or even five hundred — talents would not be much to him.

"But in the meantime he wants less than five hundred talents, my lord," Servilius said. "If his need were not virtuous, I would not urge you to lend him the money half so faithfully as I am doing now."

Timon needed the money because of his excessive giving of gifts, not because of gambling or whoremongering.

"Are you speaking seriously, Servilius?" Lucius asked.

"On my soul, I swear that it is true, sir."

"What a wicked beast was I to not be prepared for such a good opportunity when I might have shown myself to be an honorable friend!" Lucius said. "How unluckily it has happened that I should use up my money just the day before for something little, and by doing so deprive myself of a great deal of honor! Servilius, now, before the gods, I am not able to do … I am all the more beast, I say … I myself was sending to Lord Timon to borrow money, as these gentlemen can witness! But I would not, for the wealth of Athens, have done it knowing what I know now.

"Commend me bountifully to his good lordship, and I hope his honor will conceive the fairest opinion of me, although I have no power to be kind, and tell him from me that I count it one of my greatest afflictions, tell him, that I cannot gratify such an honorable gentleman.

"Good Servilius, will you befriend me so far as to use my own words when you speak to Timon?"

"Yes, sir, I shall."

"I'll keep an eye open for when I can do you a good turn, Servilius."

Servilius exited.

Lucius said to the first stranger, "What you said is true: Timon has been brought low indeed. A man who has been once denied will hardly speed. A man who has been once rebuffed will hardly prosper."

Lucius exited.

The first stranger said, "Do you see this, Hostilius?"

Hostilius, the second stranger, replied, "Yes, all too well."

"Why, this is the world's soul, and just of the same piece is every flatterer's spirit," the first stranger said.

The world's soul is the world's animating principle. Most thinkers of the time thought that it is a principle of harmony, but after observing Lucius, the first stranger thought that it is the principle of self-interest.

The first stranger continued, "Who can call him his friend that dips in the same dish?"

He was referring to sharing a meal together and dipping pieces of bread into such things as olive oil and sauces. He also was referring to Matthew 26:23: *"And he [Jesus] answered and said, He that dippeth [his] hand with me in the dish, the same shall betray me."* Jesus was referring to Judas, who betrayed him after the Last Supper, during which they had eaten together.

The first stranger continued, "I know that Timon has been like this lord's father, and kept Lucius' credit good with Timon's money, which has supported Lucius' estate; indeed, Timon's money has paid Lucius' servants their wages. Lucius never drinks without one of Timon's silver goblets treading upon his lip. And yet — oh, see the monstrousness of man when he appears in an ungrateful shape! — Lucius refuses to give to Timon, in proportion to Lucius' wealth, what charitable men give to beggars."

The third stranger said, "Religion groans at it."

The first stranger said, "As for my own part, I never fed on Timon in my life, and never have any of his bounties come to me to mark me as his friend, yet I protest that, because of his very noble mind, illustrious virtue, and honorable and moral conduct, had Timon's troubles made it necessary for him to ask for help from me, I would have used my wealth to make a donation to him — and I should have sent to him in reply to his request for a loan the best half of my wealth. That's how much I love Timon's heart. But I perceive that men must learn now to dispense with pity, for policy sits above conscience. Men must be without pity because self-interest rules conscience."

Sempronius and one of Timon's servants were speaking together in a room in Sempronius' house.

"Must Timon trouble me with his problems — hmm! — before all others?" Sempronius complained. "He might have tried Lord Lucius or Lucullus, and now Ventidius, whom he redeemed from prison, is wealthy, too. All these men owe their estates to Timon."

Sempronius was saying that he was upset because Timon had approached him first for help.

"My lord, they have all been touched and have been found base metal, for they have all denied him a loan," Timon's servant said.

Timon's servant was using a metaphor. Those three men had been tested with a touchstone, which showed that they were made of base metal rather than precious metal. To find out whether a metal was precious — gold or silver — or was base and of low value, it was rubbed on a touchstone. The color left on the touchstone showed whether the metal was precious or base.

"What!" Sempronius said. "Have they denied him a loan? Have Ventidius and Lucullus denied him a loan? And does he now send you to me to ask for a loan? Three? Hmm! It shows that he has very little friendship for me and he has very little good judgment in him. Must I be his last refuge! His friends, like physicians, thrive and then give him over. Must I take the cure upon me?"

He was comparing Ventidius, Lucullus, and Lucius to physicians who thrive by taking their patients' money and then give the patients up for dead.

Sempronius continued, "He has much disgraced me by doing it, by asking me last for money. I'm angry at him because he ought to have known my place: I should have been at the top of the list of people whom he could ask for a loan."

Before, he had said that he was angry when he thought that Timon had come to him first to borrow money; now, he was saying that he was angry that Timon had come to him last to borrow money.

Sempronius continued, "I see no sense in why he did not in his need come first to me for help, for in my understanding I was the first man who ever received a gift from him. And does he think so backwardly of me now, that I'll repay that gift last?

"No, I will not repay his gift last. If I did, it may prove to be a subject that causes laughter to the rest of the lords, and the lords would think that I am a fool. I would prefer that he had asked to borrow from me three times the amount he wants to borrow, as long as he had asked me first. I would prefer that for the sake of my mind because I would have such a desire to do him good.

"But now return to him, and with the faint reply of those three other lords join this answer: Who abates and lessens my honor shall not know my coin."

Sempronius exited.

Timon's servant said to himself, "Excellent! Your lordship's a splendid villain. The Devil did not know what he did when he made men politic — cunning when it comes to self-interest. The Devil crossed himself by doing it; he thwarted himself by making men his rivals in evil. And I cannot think but, in the end, the villainies of men will make the Devil appear innocent by comparison.

"How fairly this lord strives to appear foul! He takes on the appearance of virtue in order to be wicked, like those who under hot ardent zeal would set whole realms on fire. He is like a religious zealot who is willing to start a war — of such a nature is his politic, cunning self-love.

"Sempronius was my lord's best hope; now all his other hopes have fled, except only the gods. Now that his friends are dead to him, doors that were never acquainted with their locks during the many bounteous years that Timon was generous must be employed now to guard securely their master. And this is all a liberal — freely generous — course allows: Who cannot keep his wealth must keep his house. A man who cannot keep his wealth must keep inside his house so that he will not be arrested for debt."

Two of Varro's servants and one of Lucius' servants arrived outside Timon's house, where they met Titus, Hortensius, and other servants of Timon's creditors. All of them waited for Timon to come out of his house.

Varro's first servant said, "We are well met; good morning, Titus and Hortensius."

Titus replied, "The same to you, Varro's kind first servant."

"Lucius' servant!" Hortensius said. "Do we meet together?"

"Yes, and I think that one and the same business is why all of us are here," Lucius' servant replied. "The reason I am here is money."

Titus said, "So is theirs and ours."

Philotus walked up to the others.

Lucius' servant said, "And Sir Philotus, too!"

The "Sir" was a joke, not a real title.

"Good day to all of you," Philotus said.

Lucius' servant said, "Welcome, good brother. What do you think the time is?"

"The hour hand of the clock is laboring to reach nine," Philotus replied.

"Is it that late?" Lucius' servant said.

"Hasn't Timon, the lord I am waiting to see, been seen yet?" Philotus asked.

"Not yet," Lucius' servant replied.

"I wonder about this," Philotus said. "Timon was accustomed to rise and shine at seven."

"Yes, but the days are grown shorter with him," Lucius' servant replied. "You must consider that a prodigal course is like the course of the Sun — days that are long in the summer grow short in the winter in the northern hemisphere — but it is not, like the Sun's, recoverable. The Sun's appearance during winter is less long than its appearance during summer. However, summer will return and the Sun will return to its old course across the sky and shine longer on the Earth. I fear that it is deepest winter in Lord Timon's moneybag; that is, one may reach deep into it, and yet find little. It is like an animal digging in the winter snow for food; the animal may dig deep but find little food."

"I share your fear that Timon's moneybag lacks anything to fill it," Philotus said.

"I'll teach you how to observe and interpret a strange event," Titus said. "Your lord sends now for money from Timon."

Hortensius replied, "That is very true, he does."

"And your lord is wearing jewels now that Timon gave to him, and that is the reason that I am waiting for Timon to give me money. Timon borrowed money from my lord to give jewels to your lord, and because of that Timon is in debt and I am waiting for him to pay the debt."

"It is against my heart," Hortensius replied. "I don't like it, and I wish that it were not true."

Lucius' servant said, "Note how strange this is — it shows that Timon because of this must pay more than he owes. It is as if your lord should wear rich jewels and send for the money that was needed to pay for the jewels."

"I'm tired of this task, as the gods can witness," Hortensius said. "I know my lord has spent part of Timon's wealth, and now my lord's ingratitude makes his trying to get money from Timon worse than stealthy stealing."

Varro's first servant said, "You are right. The debt my lord is trying to collect is three thousand crowns. What is the debt that your lord is trying to collect?"

Lucius' servant replied, "Five thousand crowns."

Varro's first servant said, "It is a very large amount, and it seems by the sum that your master's confidence in Timon was above my master's confidence that Timon would repay the loan, or else, surely, the amount of money that my master lent Timon would have equaled what your master lent him."

Flaminius came outside Timon's house.

Titus said, "He is one of Lord Timon's servants."

Lucius' servant said, "Flaminius! Sir, may I have a word with you? Please, is your lord ready to come outside?"

"No, indeed, he is not," Flaminius replied.

"We are waiting for him," Titus said. "Please, tell him that."

"I need not tell him that," Flaminius said. "He knows you are very diligent in seeking him."

Flaminius exited.

Flavius came onto the scene. Seeing the creditors' servants, he attempted to leave without being seen. He held up his cloak to partially hide his face.

Lucius' servant said, "Look! Isn't that man holding his cloak up to muffle his face Timon's steward? He is going away in a cloud."

The cloud was a cloud of despair, and going away in a cloud also meant disappearing; in this case, Flavius was trying to hide his face so that he could leave without his master's creditors recognizing him.

Lucius' servant continued, "Call to him! Call to him!"

Titus said to Flavius, "Do you hear us, sir?"

Varro's second servant said, "By your leave, sir —"

Letting his cloak fall away from his face, Flavius asked, "What do you ask of me, my friend?"

"We are waiting here for certain amounts of money, sir," Titus said.

"Yes, you are," Flavius said. "If money were as certain as your waiting, it would be sure enough. Why didn't you bring your sums and bills when your false masters were eating my lord's food? Then they could smile and fawn upon his debts and take the interest — the food — into their gluttonous mouths. You are doing yourselves wrong by making me angry. Let me pass quietly. Believe it, my lord and I have made an end; I have no more sums to reckon in his accounts, and he has no more money to spend."

Lucius' servant said, "Yes, but this answer will not serve. This answer is not good enough."

Flavius muttered, "If it will not serve, it is not as base as any of you because you serve knaves."

Flavius went inside Timon's house.

Varro's first servant said, "What did his cashiered — fired — 'worship' mutter?"

He used the word "worship," which was used to refer to a man worthy of respect, sarcastically; he was angry at Flavius.

"It doesn't matter," Varro's second servant said. "He's poor, and that's revenge enough. Who can speak more critically than a man who has no house to put his head in? Such a man may rail against and criticize great buildings."

Servilius came out of Titus' house.

Titus said, "Oh, here's Servilius; now we shall know some answers to our questions."

"If I might persuade you, gentlemen, to return at some other hour, I would derive much benefit from it," Servilius said, "for I swear that my lord leans wondrously to discontent and unhappiness. His cheerful temper has forsaken him; he is not healthy, and he stays in his room."

Lucius' servant said, "Many who stay in their homes are not sick, and if his health is that far gone, I think that he should all the sooner pay his debts so that when he dies he will have a clear path to the gods."

"Good gods!" Servilius said.

"We cannot take this for an answer to our demand for money, sir," Titus said.

From inside Timon's house, Flaminius shouted, "Servilius, help!"

He then shouted to Timon, "My lord! My lord!"

Enraged, Timon came out of his house. Flaminius followed him.

"Are my doors opposed against my passage through them to go outside?" Timon said. "Have I been always free, and must my house now be my confining enemy, my jail? This place where I have given feasts, does it now, like all Mankind, show me an iron heart?"

Lucius' servant said, "Present your bill now, Titus."

"My lord, here is my bill," Titus said to Timon.

"Here's mine," Lucius' servant said.

"And mine, my lord," Hortensius said.

Both of Varro's servants said, "And ours, my lord."

Philotus said, "Here are all our bills."

One meaning of "bill" was a long-handled weapon with an axe-head at one end.

Timon said, "Knock me down with your bills. Cleave me in half all the way to my belt."

Lucius' servant said, "It's a pity, my lord."

"Cut my heart into sums of money," Timon replied.

Titus' servant said, "The sum of money I need is fifty talents."

"I will pay it with my blood," Timon replied. "Count out each drop of my blood."

Lucius' servant said, "The sum of money I need is five thousand crowns, my lord."

"Five thousand drops of my blood will pay that," Timon said.

He then asked Varro's two servants, "How much do you need? And you?"

Varro's two servants said, "My lord —"

Timon interrupted, "— tear me to pieces, take all of me, and may the gods fall upon you!"

Timon went back inside his house.

Hortensius said, "Truly, I see that our masters may throw their caps at their money: They will never get their money back. These debts may well be called desperate ones because a madman owes them."

All of the people trying to get money from Titus exited.

Inside his house, Timon said to himself, "They have even made me be out of breath because of my anger, the slaves. Creditors? They are Devils!"

Flavius said, "My dear lord —"

Not hearing him, Timon said to himself, "I have an idea. I wonder if it will work."

"My lord —" Flavius said.

"I'll do it," Timon said.

He called, "My steward!"

Flavius replied, "Here I am, my lord."

"So opportunely?" Timon asked. "Go and invite all of my friends again, Lucius, Lucullus, and Sempronius, all, sirrah, all. I'll once more feast the rascals."

"Sirrah" was a word used to address a man of lower status than the speaker.

"Oh, my lord," Flavius said. "You say that only because your soul is confused and distracted. Not enough food is left to furnish even a moderate table."

"Don't you worry about that," Timon said. "Go. I order you to invite them all to a feast here. I will let in the tide of knaves once more; my cook and I will provide the feast."

Senators were meeting in the Senate House of Athens. They were discussing the punishment of a soldier who served under Alcibiades. The soldier had gotten drunk, quarreled with another man, and killed him.

The first Senator said to the second Senator, "My lord, you have my vote for it; the crime is bloodthirsty; it is necessary he should die. Nothing emboldens sin as much as mercy."

"That is very true," the second Senator said. "The law shall crush him."

Alcibiades and some attendants entered.

Alcibiades greeted the Senators, "May honor, health, and compassion be characteristics of the Senate!"

The first Senator asked, "What do you want, Captain?"

"I am a humble suitor to your virtuous selves," Alcibiades said. "Pity is the virtue of the law, and none except tyrants use the law cruelly. It pleases time and fortune to lie heavy upon a friend of mine, who, in hot blood, has stepped into the jurisdiction of the law, which is past depth to those who, without heed, plunge into it.

"He is a man, setting his fate aside — the fate that made him do what he did — of comely virtues. Nor did he blemish his deed with cowardice — an honor in him that makes up for his fault — for with a noble fury and fair spirit, seeing his reputation stained to death, he opposed his foe, and with such sober and hardly noticeable passion he controlled his anger before it was spent that it was as if he had simply made a point in an argument."

The deed committed was serious enough that the Senators had considered it a capital crime — one that would be punished with death. Alcibiades was trying to make it seem much less serious than that.

The first Senator replied, "You are making too forced a paradox as you strive to make an ugly deed look fair. Your words have taken such pains as if they labored to make manslaughter a lawful procedure and make fighting duels one of the acts of valor. That indeed is a bastard form of valor that came into the world when sects and factions were newly born. But the truly valiant man is one who can wisely suffer the worst that another man can say, and who can make his wrongs something external to him and wear them like his clothing, in a carefree way, and who can never take his injuries to heart. If he were to take his injuries to heart, he would put his heart in danger. If wrongs are evils that force us to kill, what folly it is to hazard life for ill! We would be risking our lives for the sake of evil."

"My lord —" Alcibiades began.

The first Senator interrupted, "— you cannot make gross sins look innocent and clear; to get revenge is not valorous, but to bear and endure wrongs is valorous."

"My lords, then, if you will, pardon me if I speak like a military Captain. Why do 'foolish' men expose themselves in battle, and not endure all threats? Should they go to sleep after being threatened, and let their foes quietly cut their throats, without opposition? If such valor is found in bearing wrongs, why do we go to wars abroad? Why then, if there is such valor in bearing, women who stay at home and bear the weight of men in the act of sex and then bear children are more valiant than soldiers who fight abroad. If bearing is valorous, then the ass who bears burdens is more of a Captain than the lion; if there is wisdom in suffering, then the felon who is weighed down with irons is wiser than the judge.

"Oh, my lords, as you are great, be good and show compassion. Who cannot condemn rashness in cold blood? To kill, I grant, is sin's most extreme outburst. But to kill in self-defense, if we take a merciful view of it, is very just.

"To be angry is impious; but what man has never been angry? Weigh this man's crime with mercy."

"You speak in vain," the second Senator said.

"In vain!" Alcibiades said. "This soldier's military service done at Lacedaemon and Byzantium is a sufficient bribe for his life."

He meant that the soldier's military service in far places ought to excuse his crime in Athens.

Hearing the word "bribe," and not liking it, the first Senator asked, "What's that?"

Alcibiades replied, "I say, my lords, this soldier has done fair service, and slain in battle many of your enemies. How full of valor did he bear himself in the last conflict, and made plenteous wounds!"

The second Senator said, "He has made too much plenty with them. He's a sworn rioter — he carouses as if he had made an oath to carouse. He has a sin — drunkenness — that often drowns him and takes his valor prisoner. If there were no foes, his crime of constant drunken carousing would be enough to overcome him."

By "If there were no foes," the second Senator meant, "If there were no civilian or military foes [whom he had killed]," but Alcibiades could easily understand it as saying, "If there were no foes of Athens." Athens was currently fighting no wars; otherwise, Alcibiades would be elsewhere, fighting in the war, and the soldier would be needed to fight in the war.

The second Senator continued, "In that beastly fury caused by drunkenness, he has been known to commit outrages and support dissension. It has been reported to us that his days are foul and his drink is dangerous."

"He dies," the first Senator said.

"That is a hard fate!" Alcibiades said. "He might have died in war, which would have been a better fate. My lords, if not for any good qualities in him — though his right arm might purchase his own time of natural life and be in debt to no one — yet, the more to move you, take my merits and join them to his, and because I know your reverend ages love security — safety and collateral — I'll pawn my victories and all my honors to you because I know that he will make good returns. If by this crime he owes the law his life, why, let the war receive it in valiant gore — let him die in battle. Law is strict, and war is no less."

"We are for law," the first Senator said. "He dies. Argue about it no more, or our displeasure will heighten. No matter whether a man is your friend or your brother, that man forfeits his own blood when he spills the blood of another."

"Must it be so?" Alcibiades said. "It must not be. My lords, I beg you, know me for who I am."

"What!" the second Senator said, outraged.

"Remember me and my deeds," Alcibiades said.

"What!" the third Senator said, outraged.

"I cannot but think that because of your old age you have forgotten me and what I have done for Athens — it could not be otherwise. That is the only reason that I should be so treated so badly — I beg you for a favor and I am denied what should be quickly granted to me. The wounds I have received in battle ache when I look at you."

"Do you dare to face our anger?" the first Senator said. "It is in few words, but it is spacious in effect. We banish you from Athens forever."

"Banish me!" Alcibiades said. "You ought to banish your dotage; you ought to banish your usury that makes the Senate ugly."

"If, after two days, you are still in Athens," the first Senator said, "you will face a more serious judgment than banishment. And, so that you will lack your reason to swell our anger, the man you want to be pardoned shall be executed immediately."

The Senators exited.

Alcibiades said to himself, "Now I pray that the gods will preserve you so that you may live to be old enough that you are nothing but bones, so that no one will want to look at you! I'm worse than mad: I have kept back their foes, while they have counted their money and lent out their coins for much interest, while I myself am rich only in large wounds. All those wounds for treatment such as this? Is this the healing ointment that the usuring Senate pours onto military Captains' wounds? Banishment! Banishment isn't so bad; I don't hate being banished. It is a worthy reason for my anger and fury and an excuse to attack Athens. I'll cheer up my discontented troops, and play for hearts to be loyal to me. It is an honor to be at odds with most lands; soldiers should tolerate as few wrongs as do the gods."

The banqueting room in Timon's house was filled with tables and busy servants as several lords, Senators, and other people entered. Musicians played.

The first lord said, "Good day to you, sir."

"I also wish a good day to you," the second lord said. "I think this honorable lord — Timon — was only testing us the other day when he wanted to borrow money."

"Upon that were my thoughts being exercised, when we met just now," the first lord said. "I hope it is not so low with him as he made it seem in the test of his various friends."

"It should not be, by the evidence of this new feast that he is hosting," the second lord said.

"I should think so," the first lord said. "Timon sent me an earnest invitation, which my many personal needs urged me to decline, but he has conjured me beyond them, and I must necessarily appear at his feast. His powers of persuasion are like those of a magician."

"In like manner was I under obligation to my pressing business, but he would not hear my excuse," the second lord said. "I am sorry that when he sent a servant to borrow money from me, my supply of money was out."

"I am sick from that grief, too, since I now understand how all things go," the first lord said, meaning that he understood now that Timon was simply testing his friends to see if they would lend him money when Timon was suffering a financial emergency.

"Every man here's in the same situation and feeling the same grief," the second lord said. "What would he have borrowed from you?"

"A thousand coins."

"A thousand coins!"

"What did he want to borrow from you?" the first lord said.

"He sent to me, sir —" the second lord began, but seeing Timon, he said, "Here he comes."

Timon and some attendants walked toward the two lords.

"From all my heart to both of you gentlemen," Timon said, "and how are you doing?"

"Always I am doing the best, when I hear good things about your lordship," the first lord said.

"The swallow does not follow summer more willingly than we follow your lordship," the second lord said.

Timon thought, *Nor more willingly leaves winter; such summer-birds are men.*

He was thinking of this proverb: Swallows, like false friends, fly away upon the approach of winter.

He said out loud, "Gentlemen, our dinner will not recompense you for this long wait. Feast your ears with the music for a while, if they will metaphysically dine on the harsh sound of the trumpet; we shall get to the feast soon."

"I hope that your lordship takes it not unkindly that when you asked me for a loan I returned to you an empty-handed messenger," the first lord said.

"Oh, sir, don't let that trouble you," Timon replied.

"My noble lord —" the second lord said.

"Ah, my good friend, what is wrong?" Timon asked.

"My most honorable lord, I am even sick from shame, that, when your lordship this other day sent to me to borrow money, I was so unfortunate a beggar that I lacked money to lend to you."

"Don't worry about it, sir," Timon said.

"If you had sent your messenger to me just two hours earlier —" the second lord said.

"Don't let it distress your brain, which ought to entertain better memories," Timon said.

He ordered his servants, "Come, bring in everything all together."

The servants brought in the feast.

The second lord said, "All covered dishes!"

The best food was served under covered dishes.

"Royal cheer, I warrant you," the first lord said. "This is food fit for a King, I bet."

A third lord who had just arrived said, "There is no reason to doubt that; if money can buy it and it is in season, it is here."

"How are you?" the first lord asked. "What's the news?"

"Alcibiades has been banished. Have you heard about it?"

"Alcibiades banished!" the other lords said.

"It is so," the third lord said. "You can be sure of it."

"What? What?" the first lord exclaimed.

"Please, tell us why he was banished," the second lord requested.

"My worthy friends, will you come closer?" Timon asked.

"I'll tell you more soon," the third lord promised. "Here's a noble feast ready."

"Timon is still the man we knew of old," the second lord said.

"Will he continue to be?" the third lord said. "Will he continue to be?"

"He has so far," the second lord said, "but time will tell truth — and so —"

"I understand," the third lord said.

They were a little cautious; Timon had recently asked to borrow money from them. Would he do so again?

Timon said, "Each man go to his stool with that same eagerness as he would go to the lips of his mistress. Your diet of food shall be in all places alike. Let's not make a City feast of it and let the food cool before we can agree upon who shall sit in the first place, the place of honor. Sit, sit."

In this society, people sat on stools. Only a very high-ranking person would be offered a chair. A City feast was a formal feast in London with the higher-ranking people sitting at the head of the table and people of lower status sitting lower. At a City feast the best food would be placed at the head of the table, but at Timon's feast everyone was to be served the same diet of food.

Timon said, "The gods require our thanks."

He prayed, "You great benefactors, sprinkle our society with thankfulness. As for your own gifts, make yourselves praised, but always reserve some gifts to give later, lest you deities be despised because you have no more gifts to give. And keep something back for yourself so that you are not despised because you have nothing. Lend to each man enough, so that one man need not lend to another; as you know, if your godheads asked to borrow money from men, men would forsake the gods. Make the food be loved more than the man who gives it. Let no assembly of twenty men be without a score — twenty — of villains. If twelve women sit at the table, let a dozen of them be — what women are. Gods, concerning the rest of your foes — the Senators of Athens, together with the common rabble of people — be aware that what is amiss in them makes them suitable for destruction. For these my present — and present-loving — friends, as they are to me nothing, so in nothing bless them, and to nothing are they welcome."

Timon then ordered, "Uncover the dishes, dogs, and lap."

The dishes were uncovered and found to be full of warm water.

"What does Timon mean by this?" someone said.

"I don't know," others answered.

"May you a better feast never behold, you knot of mouth-friends — you 'friends' who say that I am your friend only as long as I feed you," Timon said. "Smoke — steam that dissipates and vanishes — and lukewarm water are the perfect feast for you and the perfect representation of your friendship for me. This is Timon's last supper; I, Timon, who is adorned and spangled with your flatteries, washes your reeking villainy off, and sprinkles it in your faces."

He dipped his hands in the lukewarm water and then flung the water in the faces of his "friends."

He shouted, "Live loathed and long, you most smiling, smooth, detested parasites, you courteous destroyers, you affable wolves, you meek bears, you fools who follow fortune, you plate-friends who are friends only when given plates full of food, you flies who appear only during the good times of summer, you cap-and-knee slaves who doff your caps and bend your knees in flattery, you vapors as insubstantial as air, and you minute-jacks!"

A jack is a figure that strikes the chime on a clock. Metaphorically, a minute-jack is a time-server, an opportunist who adjusts his behavior minute by minute according to what will bring the most profit to him.

Timon continued, "May the infinite number of maladies affecting men and beasts infect you and make your skin be completely scab covered!"

A lord stood up to leave and Timon said, "What, are you going? Wait a minute! Take your medicine first — you, too — and you —"

He threw stones at his fleeing guests.

Mockingly, he said, "Stay. I will lend you money. I won't borrow any."

He threw the stones and dishes at them, scattered their hats and cloaks, and drove them out.

He shouted, "What, all in motion? All running away! Henceforth let there be no feast where a villain's not a welcome guest. Burn, house! Sink, Athens! From now on, let all men and all humanity be hated by Timon!"

He ran out of his house.

The lords re-entered Timon's house, accompanied by some late-arriving Senators.

The first lord asked, "How are you now, my lords?"

"Do you know the reason for Lord Timon's fury?" the second lord asked.

"Bah!" the third lord said. "Did you see my cap?"

A fourth lord said, "I have lost my cloak."

The first lord said, "Timon is nothing but a mad lord, and nothing but his whims sway him. He gave me a jewel the other day, and now he has beaten it out of my hat in which I was wearing it. Have you seen my jewel?"

The third lord asked, "Did you see my cap?"

"Here it is," the second lord said.

"Here lies my cloak," the fourth lord said.

"Let's stay here no longer," the first lord said.

"Lord Timon's mad," the second lord said.

"I literally feel it upon my bones," the third lord said.

"One day he gives us diamonds, the next day stones," the fourth lord said.

CHAPTER 4

— 4.1 —

Outside the wall protecting Athens, Timon said to himself, "Let me look back upon you. Oh, you wall, which girdles and keeps in those wolves, dive into the earth, and cease to be a protective fence around Athens!

"Married women, become promiscuous!

"Obedience, fail in children!

"Slaves and fools, pluck the grave, wrinkled Senators from the bench, and govern in their steads!

"Innocent virgins, convert instantly and become general filths — common whores! Have sex in front of your parents' eyes!

"Bankrupts, hold fast; rather than give back the money you borrowed, take your knives out, and cut the throats of those who trusted you!

"Indentured servants, steal! Your grave masters are sticky-fingered robbers, and the law allows them to pillage and steal.

"Maiden, go to your master's bed. Your mistress is of the brothel — she is a bawd or a whore!

"Son of sixteen, pluck the padded crutch away from your old, limping father, and then use it to beat out his brains!

"Piety and fear, devotion to the gods, peace, justice, truth, respect given to parents, peaceful nights, and neighborliness, teaching and knowledge, manners, skilled occupations, and trades, social ranks, observances, customs, and laws — may all of you decline and become your opposites, and yet allow confusion to continue to increase!

"Plagues, which are likely to happen to men, heap your powerful and infectious fevers on Athens, which is ripe to be struck!

"You cold sciatica, cripple our Senators, so that their limbs may limp as lamely as their manners.

"Lust and licentiousness, creep in the minds and marrows of our youth, so that against the stream of virtue they may strive and drown themselves in revelry!

"Itches and blisters, sow your seeds in all the Athenian bosoms, and may their crop be general leprosy! May breath infect breath, so that their society, like their friendship, may merely poison others! I'll carry nothing away from you, except nakedness, you detestable town!"

He removed a garment and threw it through the gate he had just passed through, saying, "Take you that, too, with my curses that multiply! Timon will go to the woods, where he shall find the unkindest beast kinder — more caring and showing more kinship — than Mankind."

He paused and then shouted, "May the gods destroy — hear me, all you good gods — the Athenians both within and outside that wall! And grant, as Timon grows older, that his hatred may grow to extend to the whole race of Mankind, high and low! Amen."

Flavius talked with two of Timon's servants in Timon's old house in Athens. As steward, he was the highest-ranking servant, and so it fell to him to let the other servants know that they were now out of a job. This was serious; unless the servants could find new masters, they could become destitute.

The first servant asked, "Listen, master steward. Tell us where's our master? Where's Timon? Are we ruined? Cast off and abandoned? Is nothing remaining?"

"I am sorry, my fellows," Flavius said, "but what can I say to you? Let the righteous gods record that I am as poor as you."

"Such a house broken and bankrupt!" the first servant mourned. "So noble a master fallen! All is gone! And he does not have one friend to take his misfortunate self by the arm, and go along with him!"

The second servant said, "As we turn our backs from our companion thrown into his grave, so his associates who are familiar with his buried fortunes all slink away and leave their false vows of friendship with him, like a pickpocket leaving behind an empty wallet. And Timon, his poor self now a beggar dedicated to living in the open air, with his disease of poverty that everyone shuns, walks, like contempt, alone.

"Here come more of our fellow servants."

The other servants walked over to them.

Flavius said, "We are all broken implements of a ruined house."

The third servant said, "Yet our hearts still wear Timon's livery — the distinctive clothing that identifies us as being Timon's servants. I can see that by looking at our faces; we are still colleagues, serving alike in sorrow. Our ship is leaking, and we, poor mates, stand on the sinking deck, on which we could die, hearing the surging waves threaten us. We must all depart into this sea of air. We must leave the house."

"All you good fellows, the last of my wealth I'll share among you," Flavius said. "Wherever we shall meet, for Timon's sake, let's still be colleagues; let's shake our heads, and say, as if we were a funeral bell tolling our master's misfortunes, 'We have seen better days.' Let each take some money."

The servants held back, reluctant to take some of Flavius' last remaining money.

He said, "No, all of you put out your hands. Not one word more. Thus part we rich in sorrow, but poor in money."

The servants embraced and then departed, leaving Flavius alone.

Flavius said to himself, "Oh, the fierce and drastic wretchedness that glory brings us! Who would not wish to be excluded from wealth, since riches point to misery and contempt? Who would want to be so mocked with glory? Who would want to live in what is only a dream of friendship and not the real thing? Who would want to have his pomp and ceremony and all of what makes up magnificence be only superficial, like a thin layer of paint, and like his so-called friends? Poor honest lord, brought low by his own heart, undone and ruined by his goodness! It is a strange, unusual nature when a man's worst sin is that he does too much good! Who, then, dares to be half as kind and generous as Timon again? Generosity, that makes gods, always mars men. My dearest lord was blessed, and now he is most accursed. He was rich, only to now be wretched. Timon, your great fortunes have been made your chief afflictions. Poor, kind lord! He has dashed away in rage from this ungrateful seat of monstrous friends, and he does not have with him those things that are needed to sustain his life, and he lacks the money to buy those things.

"I'll follow after him and inquire about and find out where he is. I'll always serve his desires with my best will. While I have gold, I'll be his steward still."

Flavius lacked physical gold, but as long as he had gold in his heart, he wanted to serve Timon.

Timon was living in a cave in the woods, near the seashore.

He came out of the cave and said to himself, "Oh, blessed infection-breeding Sun, draw up from the earth noxious vapors that cause things to rot. Below your sister's orbit, infect the air!"

In mythology, the sister of the Sun was the Moon. According to this society's beliefs, the Earth was the center of the universe, and whatever was under the Moon was corruptible, while the heavens were incorruptible. Timon wanted the Sun to corrupt the air in between the Earth and the Moon. Infected air would cause plague in the land under the air.

Timon continued, "Let's consider twinned brothers of one womb, whose procreation, residence in the womb, and birth scarcely makes them different. Suppose that they are put to the test by being given different fortunes; the brother with the greater fortune will scorn the brother with the lesser fortune. Let me go further and apply this to humans as a whole. Human nature, to which all afflictions lay siege, cannot bear great fortune except by being contemptuous of human nature."

People who enjoy great good fortune will come to despise people who do not enjoy great good fortune. People who enjoy great good fortune will come to believe that they are better than other people. After all, they think, I am rich, so why isn't everyone else rich? There must be something wrong with them. This applies to things other than riches — for example, fame, success, and so on.

Alexander the Great was wondrously successful, and he came to believe that he was a god.

We should keep in mind that all afflictions lay siege to human nature. Those afflictions include the seven deadly sins, of which the foremost is pride. If we could keep that in mind, we would not think that being fortunate makes us better than other people.

Timon continued, "Raise this beggar and make him successful, and make that lord lack success. If that happens, then the Senator shall be regarded with contempt as if his contemptuousness were his inheritance, and the beggar will be regarded with honor as if it were his birthright."

Successful people are honored; unsuccessful people are not. Very fortunate people can regard the two groups of people as two different species.

Timon continued, "It is the pasture that lards the brother's sides, and the lack of land that makes the other brother lean. The brother with pastureland can raise cattle that he can eat and that will make him fat."

Much success is the result of birth. In the age of primogeniture, the older brother gets the bulk of the inheritance. A twin, but younger, brother inherits little.

A person born into a middle-class, or higher, family often has a better chance of success than one born into a destitute family.

Timon continued, "Who dares, who dares, in purity of manhood — a man who is pure and morally upright — to stand upright, and say, 'This man's a flatterer'? If one man is a flatterer, then so are they all because the people on every step of fortune are flattered by the people on the step below. The learned head bows to the golden fool; an educated man bows to a fool when the fool has money. All is oblique and slanting. There's nothing level and direct in our cursed natures, except straightforward villainy. Therefore, let all feasts, societies, and throngs of men be abhorred! I, Timon, disdain all human beings, including myself. May destruction use its fangs to grab Mankind!"

He began digging with a spade and said, "Earth, give me edible roots! Whoever seeks for something better from you, season his palate with your most powerful poison!

"What is here? Gold? Yellow, glittering, precious gold? No, gods, I am no idle vow-maker. I asked for edible roots, you innocent, pure Heavens!

"This amount of gold will make black white, foul fair, wrong right, base noble, old young, and coward valiant. Ha, you gods! Why this? What is the reason for this, you gods? Why have you allowed me to find gold? Why, this amount of gold will haul your priests and servants away from your sides, and it will pluck healthy men's pillows from below their heads."

When people were dying, their pillows were taken away from under their heads to make it easier to die. The sixteenth-century *Shiltei Hagiborim* by R. Joshua Boaz argued against what he regarded as a form of what we would probably call euthanasia:

"There would appear to be grounds for forbidding the custom, practiced by some, in the case of someone who is dying and his soul cannot depart, of removing

the pillow from underneath the goses [someone who is expected to die within 72 hours] so that he will die quickly. For they say that the bird feathers in the bedding prevent the soul from leaving the body."

In some societies, people believe that a lone pigeon is an omen of death, and people believe that pigeon feathers in a pillow prolong the agony of dying, and so they remove pillows containing pigeon feathers from sickrooms.

When Timon said that gold would pluck healthy men's pillows from below their heads, he meant that gold would cause greedy people to cause healthy men to die.

Timon continued, "This yellow slave will knit and break religions, bless the accursed, make those with hoary, white leprosy adored, place thieves into positions of high status and make them equivalent to Senators on the bench in terms of rank and title, deference and the right to be knelt to, and approval and approbation.

"This gold is what makes the wappened widow wed again. She, whom those with ulcerous sores in the hospital-house would vomit at the sight of, is embalmed and preserved with golden spices until she takes on the appearance of an April day again."

Possibly, Timon was referring to two women, depending in part on the meaning of the unusual word "wappened." If the word meant "worn out," then he was perhaps referring to one woman, a worn-out widow who was afflicted with ulcerous sores.

However, if "wappened" meant either "saddened" or "frightened," then Timon could be referring to two women. The widow would be saddened by the death of a good husband or frightened by a possible marriage to a bad husband, but a man who owns gold will overcome either her sadness or her fear. In that case, the woman with ulcerous sores could be a different woman.

Timon continued, "Come, damned earth, you common whore of Mankind, which everyone treads on and plows, and which makes the rout — the disorderly mobs — of nations at odds with each other, I will make you do what is your right nature — I will make you give me edible roots."

Timon heard the sounds of marching soldiers.

"Ha! A military drum?" Timon said. "You, gold, are quick, but I'll still bury you."

The word "quick" meant "alive." Gold is alive in the sense that it can reproduce. Usurers make gold reproduce by lending it out at interest. Gold is also quick — fast — in that it is quickly spent or lost.

Timon continued, "You shall go, gold, you strong thief, when gouty keepers of you cannot stand."

Gold shall continue to move and circulate even when its gouty owners are unable to stand and when they have died.

Timon then said, "I'll keep some of you as 'earnest money' — money to use as a down payment for things that I want to happen."

He kept some of the gold and buried the rest.

To the sound of military drum and fife, Alcibiades arrived, accompanied by two whores, one on each arm. The whores were named Phrynia and Timandra.

"Who are you there?" Alcibiades asked. "Speak."

He did not recognize Timon, who was not wearing fine clothing anymore. Timon looked wild.

"I am a beast, as are you," Timon replied. "May the cankerworm gnaw your heart because you showed me again the eyes of man! I don't want to ever again see a human being!"

"What is your name? Is man so hateful to you, who are yourself a man?"

"I am Misanthropos, and I hate Mankind," Timon replied.

Misanthropos is Greek for Man-Hater.

He continued, "As for your part, I wish you were a dog, so that I might love you somewhat."

Recognizing Timon, Alcibiades said, "I know you well, but I am ignorant about what has happened to you."

"I know you, too," Timon said, "and more than that I know you, I do not desire to know. Follow your military drum away from here, and with man's blood paint the ground, red, red. Religious canons and civil laws are cruel, so then what should war be? This deadly whore of yours has in her more destruction than your sword, for all her angelic look."

Earlier, a page had given Timon a letter from the Fool's boss, the proprietor of a whorehouse, so he recognized that at least one of the women with Alcibiades was a whore.

Insulted, Phrynia said, "May your lips rot off!"

The rotting off of lips was a sign of venereal disease.

"I will not kiss you," Timon said. "That way, the rot returns to your own lips again."

In this society, people believed that one way to cure themselves of venereal disease was to pass it on to another person. By refusing to kiss Phrynia, Timon was refusing to catch her venereal disease and so she would keep it and her lips would rot.

"How came the noble Timon to this change of fortune?" Alcibiades asked.

"As the Moon does, by lacking light to give," Timon replied. "But then renew it I could not, like the Moon is able to. There were no Suns to borrow of."

The Moon lacks light of its own; it reflects the light of the Sun. Each month the Moon renews itself with a new Moon. Timon had run out of money to give away, and he had been unable to borrow more, and so now he was living in a cave.

"Noble Timon, what friendly act may I do for you?" Alcibiades asked.

"None, but to help me maintain my opinion," Timon replied.

"What friendly act would that be, Timon?"

"Promise me friendship, but perform no friendly acts for me," Timon replied. "If you will not promise to be my friend, then may the gods plague you because you are a man! If you do perform a friendly act for me, then confound you because you are a man!"

"I have heard a little about your miseries," Alcibiades said.

"You saw my miseries, when I had prosperity."

"I see your miseries now; when you had prosperity, that was a blessed time."

"Then I was as blessed as you are now — you are tied to a brace of harlots."

A brace is a pair; sometimes the word "brace" is used to refer to a pair of dogs. Timon was saying that Alcibiades was not blessed now; being with a pair of whores — aka bitches — was no blessing.

Timandra, one of the brace of harlots, asked, "Is this the Athenian minion whom the world praised so much?"

A "minion" is a darling, but the word is often used sarcastically.

"Are you Timandra?" Timon asked.

"Yes."

"Be a whore always," Timon said. "Those who use you sexually do not love you. Give them diseases in return for them giving you their lust. Make use of your lecherous hours. Season the slaves for tubs and baths. Bring down rose-cheeked youth to the tub-fast and the diet.”

In this society, a treatment for venereal disease was to soak and sweat in hot tubs and baths. During the treatment for venereal disease, people would refrain from sex (a kind of fast) and they would adhere to a special diet, including refraining from eating rich food.

“Hang you, monster!” Timandra said.

“Pardon him, sweet Timandra,” Alcibiades said, “for his wits are drowned and lost in his calamities. I have but little gold of late, splendid Timon, the lack whereof daily makes revolt in my poverty-stricken band of soldiers. I have heard, and grieved over, how cursed Athens, mindless of your worth, forgetting your great deeds, when neighbor nations, except for your sword and your fortune, would have defeated and trod upon them —”

“Please, strike up your drum, and get you gone,” Timon said.

“I am your friend, and I pity you, dear Timon.”

“How do you pity a man whom you cause trouble? I prefer to be alone.”

“Why, fare you well,” Alcibiades said. “Here is some gold for you.”

“Keep it,” Timon said. “I cannot eat it.”

“When I have laid proud Athens in ruins on a heap —”

Timon interrupted, “Are you warring against Athens?”

“Yes, Timon, and I have cause to war against Athens.”

“May the gods destroy all the Athenians when you conquer them, and may they destroy you afterward, when you have conquered them!”

“Why me, Timon?”

“Because you were born to conquer my country by killing villains,” Timon replied.

Timon wanted everyone to be destroyed, including those who destroyed his enemies.

Taking out some of his gold, he said to Alcibiades, “Put away your gold. Go on, put it away. Here’s gold — go on, take it.”

Alcibiades did not take it.

Timon continued, “Be like a planetary plague, when Jove decides to hang his poison in the sick air over some high-viced city.”

In this society, people believed that Jupiter, aka Jove, King of the gods, caused plague by poisoning the air.

Timon continued, "When you conquer Athens, don't let your sword skip even one person.

"Don't pity an honored, aged man because he has a white beard — he is a usurer.

"Strike down for me the counterfeit matron. It is her clothing only that is honest and chaste — she herself is a bawd.

"Don't let the virgin's cheek make soft your trenchant sword; for those milk-paps, those nipples, that through the lattice-work of the bodice bore at men's eyes, are not written down in the list that is on the leaf of pity, but write them down in the list of horrible traitors."

During the conquest of a city, rapes occur. In saying not to let a virgin's cheek make soft a sword because the man with a hard "sword" feels pity for the virgin, Timon was advocating the rape of virgins. But by referring to milk-paps — milk-producing nipples — he was also saying that the "virgins" and virgins were likely to be now or to be soon mothers rather than virgins.

Timon continued, "Don't spare the babe, whose dimpled smiles arouse the mercy of fools. Think that the babe is a bastard whom the oracle has ambiguously pronounced the throat shall cut, and cut the babe into tiny bits without remorse."

An oracle is a priest or a priestess through whom a god can make prophecies. Oracles of ancient times were often ambiguous. In a famous case, Croesus, King of Lydia, wondered whether to attack the mighty Kingdom of Persia, so he went to the oracle of Delphi and sought advice. The oracle replied, "If you attack Persia, a mighty Kingdom will fall." Croesus attacked Persia, and a mighty Kingdom did fall — the mighty Kingdom of Lydia.

"The throat shall cut" is ambiguous. Whose throat? Shall the babe grow up and cut Alcibiades' throat? Or shall Alcibiades cut the babe's throat? Timon was advising Alcibiades not to wait, but to cut the babe's throat now and be safe. Pretend that an oracle has spoken, and then act to keep yourself safe.

Timon continued, "Swear against objections. Put metaphorical armor on your ears and on your eyes; put tested and proven armor on so that the yells of mothers, nor maidens, nor babes, nor the sight of bleeding priests wearing holy vestments, shall pierce the armor even a tiny bit."

He gave Alcibiades some gold and said, "There's gold to pay your soldiers. Cause much destruction, and once your fury against Athens is spent, may you yourself be destroyed! Speak no more to me! Leave!"

"Do you still have gold?" Alcibiades asked, surprised. "I'll take the gold you give me, but I won't take all of your advice to me."

He took the gold.

"Whether you do, or you don't, may Heaven's curse be upon you!" Timon said.

Phrynia and Timandra, the two whores, said, "Give us some gold, good Timon. Do you have more?"

"I have enough to make a whore forswear her trade and to become a bawd and make other women whores," Timon said.

With the gold that Timon had, a whore could set herself up as the proprietor of a whorehouse and let other women do the whoring. No doubt Timon believed that if the new whores were recently sweet, young virgins, so much the better.

He continued, "Hold up, you sluts, your aprons mountant."

He wanted the two whores to hold their aprons up so that they could catch the gold he threw to them. The aprons were mountant — always being lifted — because the whores would lift their dresses so the whores could be mounted and make money.

Timon continued, "You are not oathable, although, I know, you'll swear, terribly swear into strong shudders and to Heavenly agues the immortal gods who hear you."

The two whores were not oathable because although they were very willing to swear oaths to the gods, they could not be trusted to keep them. "Strong shudders" and "Heavenly agues" are characteristics of orgasms and of venereal diseases. An ague is a fever, sickness, or shaking caused by a fever.

Timon continued, "Spare your oaths, I'll trust to your personal characters: Once a whore, always a whore. Be whores always. When you meet a man whose pious breath seeks to convert you, be strong in whoredom."

In Ephesians 6:10 Saint Paul advises, *"Finally, my brethren, be strong in the Lord, and in the power of his might."*

Timon continued, "Allure him, burn him up with lust and venereal disease. Let your enclosed fire dominate his smoke, and you two don't be turncoats."

An enclosed fire is a vagina. Smoke is the vapor of words not believed by the person who speaks them. Some people blow smoke up a place near an enclosed fire.

He continued, "Yet may your pain-sick mounts be quite contrary to your best interests, and thatch your poor thin roofs with burdens you get from the dead — including some who were hanged."

Venereal disease was thought to cause baldness. The burdens of the dead referred to hair harvested from corpses and made into wigs.

Timon continued, "It doesn't matter — wear the wigs, betray your customers with them by looking attractive so men will have sex with you. Always be a whore. Apply cosmetics to your face so thickly that a horse could sink in the mire on your face. May you have a plague of wrinkles you have to cover up with cosmetics!"

"Pain-sick mounts" referred to sexual mountings that caused the pain of venereal disease. However, Timon sometimes muttered, and he may have said, "pain-sick months," which might be a reference to the months a whore could spend in prison, during which time she might acquire hair from corpses to use to make herself a wig and/or to sell in order to get money to buy cosmetics. However, the usual punishment for prostitution was a whipping.

What is clear is that Timon wanted the two whores to cause men to suffer from venereal disease, and he wanted the whores to also suffer from venereal disease.

Phrynia and Timandra said, "Well, give us more gold. What do you want us to do then? Believe that we'll do anything for gold."

Timon replied, "I want you to sow wasting venereal diseases in the bones of men and make them hollow. I want you to strike their sharp shins, and mar men's spurring."

The spurring referred to riding, both of horses and of whores.

He continued, "Crack the lawyer's voice, so that he may never more plead a false legal case, nor sound his quibbles shrilly.

"Hoar — make white with disease — the priest, who scolds against the nature of flesh, and does not believe what he himself says.

"Down with the nose. Down with it flat. Take the bridge entirely away from the nose of the man who, hunting to provide for his particular, individual good, loses the scent of the general good."

Venereal disease destroyed the bridge of the nose, thereby making the nose flat.

Timon continued, "Make curly-headed ruffians bald, and let the unscarred braggarts of the war derive some pain from you."

Unscarred braggarts were cowards; in contrast to cowards, brave men who fought in battles tended to have scars.

He continued, "Plague all so that your activity may defeat and destroy the source of all erection."

He threw more gold onto their laps and said, "There's more gold. May you damn others, and let this damn you, and may all of you find your graves in ditches!"

Phrynia and Timandra said, "Give us more advice and more money, generous Timon."

"More whore and more mischief first," Timon said. "I have given you a down payment for what I want from you."

"Strike up the drum and let us march towards Athens!" Alcibiades said. "Farewell, Timon. If I thrive well, I'll visit you again."

"If I hope well, I'll never see you any more," Timon said.

"I never did you harm."

"Yes, you did. You spoke well of me."

"Do you call that harm?"

"Men daily find that it is," Timon replied.

Luke 6:26 states, "*Woe be to you when all men speak well of you: for so did their fathers to the false prophets.*"

He continued, "Go away from here, and take your beagles with you."

"Beagles" was a slang word for whores.

Alcibiades said, "We are only offending him. Strike the drum and let's leave!"

The drum sounded, and everyone except Timon exited.

Alone, Timon said to himself, "It's odd that my human nature, which is sick of man's unkindness, should still continue to get hungry!"

He started digging into the ground, hoping to find edible roots.

He continued, "Earth, you common mother, your immeasurable womb prolifically gives birth to all, and your infinite breast feeds all. Earth, the same essence that creates your child, arrogant man, who is puffed up with pride, also engenders and gives birth to the black toad and blue adder, the gilded newt and eyeless poisonous worm, along with all the abhorred births below the pure Heaven where the Sun's life-giving fire shines. Earth, give to me, whom all your human sons hate, from forth your plenteous bosom, one poor edible root!

"Dry up your fertile and fruitful womb, and let it no more give birth to ungrateful man! May your belly grow large with tigers, dragons, wolves, and bears! May it teem with new monsters, whom your upward face has to the marbled mansion — the cloud-laced Heaven — above never presented!"

His spade upturned an edible root, and Timon said, "Oh, a root! I give you my dear thanks!"

He paused, and then he continued with his prayer, "Dry up your marrows, vines, and plow-torn fields, from which ungrateful man, with liquorish drinks and fatty morsels of food, greases and corrupts his pure mind, so that from it all consideration for others and ability to think slips!"

Marrows are the edible insides of plants and fruits.

Apemantus the philosopher appeared, and Timon said, "Another man is visiting me? It's a plague, a plague!"

"I was told to come here," Apemantus said. "Men report that you are imitating my manners, and acting the way I act."

"The reason for it, then, is that you do not keep a dog, whom I would imitate," Timon said. "May you contract a wasting disease!"

"This is in you a nature that is only an infection; it is not intrinsic in you because you were not born with it," Apemantus said. "This is a poor unmanly melancholic depression sprung from a change in fortune. Why do you have this spade? Why are you in this place? Why are you wearing this slave-like clothing? And why do you have these looks of sorrow?

"Your flatterers still wear silk, drink wine, lie on soft beds, hug their diseased, perfumed mistresses, and have forgotten that Timon ever existed. Don't shame these woods by putting on the cunning of a carping critic.

"Instead, become a flatterer now, and seek to thrive by doing that which others did that has undone you. Bend your knee and bow so deeply that the breath of the man whom you flatter will blow off your cap; praise his most vicious strain of character, and call it excellent.

"You were flattered like that. You gave your ears like bartenders who bid welcome to knaves and everyone else who approached them. Bartenders welcome all men. It is very just that you turn rascal — you are like a young, weak deer. If you had wealth again, human rascals would get it. Do not assume my likeness."

"If I were like you, I would throw myself away," Timon said.

"You cast away yourself by being like yourself," Apemantus replied. "You were a madman for so long, and now you are a fool. Do you think that the bleak air, your boisterous personal servant, will warm your shirt by the fire before you put it on? Will these mossy trees, which have outlived the long-lived eagle, act like pages and follow you at your heels, and skip to perform any errand you point out for them to do? Will the cold brook, crystalized with ice, make you a caudle — a warm medicinal drink — to take away the bad taste you have in your mouth when you wake up with a hangover?

"Call the creatures whose naked natures are continually exposed to the spite of vengeful Heaven; call the creatures whose bare unprotected trunks, exposed to the conflicting elements, encounter raw nature. Tell them — animals and trees — to flatter you. Oh, you shall find —"

Timon interrupted, "— that you are a fool. Depart and leave me alone."

"I love you better now than I ever did."

"I hate you worse."

"Why?"

"You flatter misery."

"I don't flatter you; instead, I say that you are a caitiff," Apemantus said. "You are a miserable wretch."

"Why do you seek me out?"

"To vex you."

"That is always the work of a villain or a fool," Timon said. "Does vexing me please you?"

"Yes."

"Then you must be a knave, too."

"If you had adopted this sour and cold manner of living in order to castigate your pride, it would be well done," Apemantus said, "but you act like this because you are forced to. You would be a courtier again if you were not a beggar.

"Willing misery outlives uncertain pomp and greatness."

According to Apemantus, a person who willingly embraces poverty outlives a person who has good fortune but who can at any time lose it.

He continued, "Willing misery is crowned before and achieves glory sooner than the person who has good fortune but who can at any time lose it.

"The one person keeps trying to get his fill of material things, but is never completely full. The other person, who wishes for little, can fulfill his wishes.

"The person who has great fortune, but is unhappy, has a distracted and most wretched existence that is worse than the existence of a person who has little fortune, but is happy.

"You should wish to die, since you are miserable."

Timon replied, "I won't accept the advice of a man who is more miserable than I am. You are a slave, whom Lady Fortune's tender arm never hugged with favor; you were bred a dog.

"Had you, like us — other wealthy men and I — from our first swaddling clothes, advanced through the sweet degrees that this brief world affords to such as may freely command its passive drudges — whores who lie passively under us — you would have plunged yourself in wholesale dissipation. You would have melted down your youth in different beds of lust. You would have never learned the icy rules that a respectable person must follow — they are icy because they cool the hot blood of unethical lust. Instead, you would have followed the sugared game — sweet sexual prey — in front of you.

"But I had the world as my confectionary, my source of sweet things. I had the mouths, the tongues, the eyes, and the hearts of men on duty, waiting to serve me. I had more men waiting to serve me than I could find employment for. These men, whom I was unable to count because there were so many and who upon me stuck as leaves stick upon an oak tree, have with one winter wind's brush fallen from their boughs and left me exposed to the natural elements, bare to every storm that blows.

"For me, who never knew anything except good fortune, to bear this is a real burden.

"In contrast, your mortal life began with suffering, and time has made you hardened to it. Why should you hate men? They never flattered you. What have you given away as gifts? If you will curse people, then you must curse your father, that poor rag, who in spite stuffed a female beggar and put stuff in her that made her pregnant with you and made you a poor rogue. Being a poor rogue is your inheritance. Therefore, leave and be gone!

"If you had not been born the worst and least fortunate of men, you would have been a knave and flatterer."

"Are you still proud?" Apemantus asked.

"Yes, I am proud that I am not you."

"I am proud that I was no prodigal. I did not waste money the way you did."

"I am proud that I am a prodigal now," Timon replied. "If all the wealth I have were shut up in you, I would give you leave to hang it. That way, I would get rid of you and all my wealth. Get you gone."

Holding up an edible root, he said, "I wish that the whole population of Athens were in this! Thus would I eat it."

He took a big bite of the root.

"Here," Apemantus said. "I will improve your feast."

He offered Timon a medlar, a kind of apple-sized fruit that was eaten when it had partially rotted.

Ignoring the medlar, Timon said, "First mend my company by taking away yourself."

"By doing that, I shall mend my own company, by the lack of your company."

"It is not well mended that way, for it is only botched," Timon said. "Your company will be worse because you will have only your own company. If what I say is not true, then I wish that it were true."

"What would you have sent to Athens?" Apemantus asked, meaning what message would Timon like Apemantus to take back to the Athenians.

"I would have you sent there in a whirlwind so it can cause destruction to Athens. But if you will, tell the people in Athens that I have gold."

Timon knew that this news would make the Athenians envious of him, thereby making them unhappy.

He showed Apemantus the gold and said, "Look, what I say is true."

"Here is no use for gold."

"Here is the best and truest use for gold," Timon said. "For here it sleeps and does no hired harm. Here it is not used to bribe and corrupt."

"Where do you lie at night, Timon?"

"Under that which is above me — the sky. Where do you eat during the day, Apemantus?"

"Where my stomach finds food — or, rather, where I eat it."

"I wish that poison were obedient and knew my mind!"

"What would you do with poison?" Apemantus asked.

"Use it to season and spice your food."

"The middle of humanity you never knew; you knew only the extremity of both ends," Apemantus said. "You knew what it is like to be very rich, and then you knew what it is like to be very poor. When you wore gilt clothing and perfume, people mocked you for your excessive fastidiousness. Now, in your rags you know no fastidiousness, but you are despised because you lack gilt and perfume."

He again offered Timon food and said, "There's a medlar for you, eat it."

"On what I hate I feed not."

"Do you hate a medlar?"

"Yes, although it looks like you," Timon said.

This, of course, was an insult. Timon was saying that Apemantus' face looked like a half-rotten apple-sized fruit.

"If you had hated meddlers sooner, you would have loved yourself better now. Have you ever known a spendthrift man who was loved after his money ran out?"

"Have you ever known a man without money who was loved?" Timon asked.

"Myself," Apemantus replied.

"I understand you; you had some money that allowed you to keep a dog."

"To what things in the world can you most closely compare your flatterers?"

"Women are the closest, but men — men are the things themselves. Women are like flatterers, but men are flatterers," Timon replied, and then he asked, "What would you do with the world, Apemantus, if it lay in your power?"

"Give it to the beasts, so I would be rid of the men. The world would no longer contain men, and the beasts would be rewarded with the world for their having gotten rid of the men."

"Would you have yourself fall in the confusion of men, and remain a beast with the beasts?" Timon asked.

One kind of "fall" is to "descend." Apemantus could descend from being a man to being a beast. One kind of "fall in" is to "line up with." Apemantus could line up with the beasts and help them to destroy men.

"Yes, Timon," Apemantus replied.

Timon said, "That is a beastly ambition, which I hope that the gods grant to you. If you were the lion, the fox would beguile you."

He was referring to one of Aesop's fables, in which an elderly lion wanted a fox to help him get something to eat by luring a stag into his cave. The fox went to the stag and said, "The lion, King of the wilderness, is dying, and he wants you to be King after him. I am going to see the lion, and you ought to come, too, in order to be with him in his last moments of life." The stag went with the fox to the lion's cave, and the lion tried to kill the stag but managed only to make bloody one of the stag's ears before the stag succeeded in fleeing. The fox went after the stag, who reprimanded him for trying to get him killed, but the fox said, "You are mistaken. The lion wasn't trying to kill you; he was trying to whisper some important information in your ears. You panicked and jumped around, and you are the reason your ear is bloody. After much persuading, the stag returned to the lion's cave with the fox, and this time the lion succeeded in killing the stag. The lion feasted on the stag and then slept, and while the lion slept the fox ate the stag's brains. When the lion woke up and wanted to eat the stag's brains, the fox said, "You won't find any brains. Any stag dumb enough to walk twice into a lion's cave doesn't have any brains."

Timon continued, "If you were the lamb, the fox would eat you."

This may be a relevant fable: A fox that was hungry for breakfast saw a lamb in a stream. The lamb was so young and innocent that the fox wanted a justification for killing and eating the lamb. The fox first complained that the lamb was stirring up mud in the water, making it undrinkable, but the lamb pointed out that the fox was upstream, where the water was clear. The fox then complained that the lamb had said bad things about him last year, but the lamb pointed out that it had been born only recently. The fox then said, "If it wasn't you that said bad things about me, then it was one of your family," and he killed and ate the lamb.

Timon continued, "If you were the fox, the lion would suspect you, when perchance you were accused by the ass."

Apparently, this was a reference to another folk tale or fable, perhaps this one: An ass and a fox were walking together when they met a lion, and they were afraid that the lion would kill and eat them. The fox said to the ass, "Wait here, and I will go to the lion and convince him not to kill and eat us." The ass agreed, and the fox approached the lion and made a deal with it out of the hearing of the ass. The deal was that the fox would find a way to trap the ass so that the lion could kill and eat it, and the lion would leave the fox alone. The lion agreed, and the fox managed to trick the ass so that it fell into a pit that was so deep that the ass could not climb out but not so deep that the lion could not jump in and out. But the ass said to the lion, "The fox tricked me, and if you allow it to live, the fox will trick you, too." So the lion killed and ate the fox, and later the lion killed and ate the ass.

Timon continued, "If you were the ass, your dullness would torment you, and all the time you lived you would fear becoming a breakfast to the wolf.

"If you were the wolf, your greediness would afflict you, and often you would hazard your life for your dinner.

"If you were the unicorn, pride and wrath would confound you and make your own self the conquest of your fury."

He was referring to the tradition that unicorns so hated lions that the unicorn would rush at a lion in an attempt to use its horn to spear the lion as it attempted to escape by climbing a tree. Often the lion successfully climbed the tree and the unicorn's horn would be deeply embedded in the trunk of the tree, and then the lion would jump out of the tree and kill the unicorn.

Timon continued, "If you were a bear, you would be killed by the horse.

"If you were a horse, you would be seized by the leopard.

"If you were a leopard, you would be closely related to the lion and the spots — the moral blemishes — of the lion would sit in judgment like jurors on your life. They would bear false witness against you. All your safety would lie in flight to a faraway place, and your best defense would be absence."

"What beast could you be that is not subject to a beast?

"And what a beast are you already, who does not see your loss if you were transformed into a beast?"

Apemantus replied, "If you could please me with speaking to me, you might have hit upon it here and now when you call me a beast and not a man."

He paused and then added, "The commonwealth of Athens has become a forest of beasts."

"How has the ass broken the wall, that you are out of the city?" Timon asked.

"From yonder are coming a poet and a painter," Apemantus replied. He knew that as soon as they heard that Timon had gold they would plan to visit Timon.

He added, "May the plague of company light upon you! I fear to catch that plague and so I leave. When I don't know what else to do, I'll see you again."

"When there is nothing living except you, you shall be welcome," Timon replied. "I had rather be a beggar's dog than Apemantus."

"You are the cap of all the fools alive," Apemantus said. "You are the best example of a fool."

"I wish that you were clean enough for me to spit upon!" Timon said.

"A plague on you!" Apemantus said. "You are too bad to curse."

"All villains who stand beside you are pure and innocent in comparison."

"There is no leprosy except what you speak —"

"— if I say your name," Timon interrupted. "I would beat you, but I would infect my hands."

"I wish my tongue could rot your hands off!"

"Go away, you offspring of a mangy dog!" Timon said. "My anger that you are alive is killing me. I swoon because I see that you are alive."

"I wish that you would burst!" Apemantus said.

"Go away, you tedious rogue! I am sorry I shall lose a stone because of you."

Timon threw a stone at Apemantus, who said, "Beast!"

"Slave!"

"Toad!"

"Rogue! Rogue! Rogue!" Timon said. "I am sick of this false world, and I will love nothing except only the mere necessities on it. So then, Timon, immediately prepare your grave, for death is a necessity. Lie where the light foam of the sea may beat your gravestone daily. Make your epitaph, so that even when you are dead you can laugh at others' lives."

He said to the gold, "Oh, you sweet King-killer, and dear divorce between blood-related son and sire! You bright defiler of Hymen, the god of marriage's purest bed! You valiant war-god Mars, who committed adultery with Venus!

You ever young, fresh, loved, and delicate wooer, whose blush — shine — thaws the consecrated snow that lies on the virgin goddess Diana's lap! Gold, you can convince even Diana not to be a virgin! You visible god that sexually welds firmly together impossibilities, and makes them kiss! Gold, you speak with every language, to every purpose! Oh, you touchstone — you tester — of hearts! Believe that your slave — Mankind — rebels, and by your virtue set all men into ruinous conflict, so that beasts may have the world as their empire!"

"I wish that it would be so!" Apemantus said. "But not until I am dead. I'll tell people in Athens that you have gold. People will throng to you shortly."

"Throng to me!" Timon said.

"Yes."

"Show me your back, please," Timon requested. "Leave."

"Live, and love your misery," Apemantus said.

"Long may you live, be miserable, and die miserably," Timon replied.

Apemantus left.

Timon said to himself, "I am quit of him."

He saw some men coming toward him, so he withdrew and said to himself, "More things like men! Eat, Timon, and hate them."

The men, who were bandits, did not see Timon withdraw.

The first bandit said, "How can he have this gold? It is some poor fragment of his former fortune, some slender scrap of what he had left. His complete lack of gold, and his falling away from his friends, drove him into this melancholy."

"It is rumored that he has a mass of treasure," the second bandit said.

"Let us make a trial attempt to get his gold by simply asking for it," the third bandit said. "If he does not care for it, he will supply us with it easily — he will give it to us. But if he covetously keeps it for himself, how shall we get it?"

"It's true that it would be hard to get in that case," the second bandit said. "He does not carry the gold on his person; the gold is hidden."

Seeing Timon, the first bandit asked, "Isn't that him?"

"Where?" the third bandit asked.

"He fits the description," the second bandit said.

"It is him," the third bandit said. "I recognize him."

"May God save you, Timon," the bandits said.

"How are you, thieves?" Timon asked.

"We are soldiers, not thieves," the bandits replied.

They may have been some soldiers serving under Alcibiades, or they may have deserted Alcibiades' army.

"You are both, and you are women's sons," Timon said.

"We are not thieves, but we are men who much do want," the bandits replied.

The word "want" meant either "desire" or "lack," or sometimes both.

"Your greatest want is that you want much food," Timon said. "Why should you want? Look, the earth has edible roots. Within a mile are a hundred springs of water. The oaks bear acorns. The scarlet roses bear the fruit called hips. The generous housewife, Mother Nature, on each bush lays her complete menu before you. Want! Why should you want?"

"We cannot live on grass, on berries, and on water, as beasts and birds and fishes do," the first bandit said.

"Nor can you live on the beasts themselves and on the birds and fishes," Timon said. "You must eat men. Yet I must give you thanks because you are confessed thieves and because you do not work in holier shapes, for there is boundless theft in limited professions. Even legal professions have much theft in them."

Timon gave them some gold and said, "Rascal thieves, here's gold. Go, suck the subtle blood of the grape until you get drunk and the high fever makes your blood boil until it is froth, and so die from alcoholism-induced fever, thereby escaping death by hanging. Do not trust the physician; his antidotes are poison, and he slays more people than you rob. He takes his patients' wealth as well as their lives. Do villainy, do, since you confess you do it, like workmen — as if you were skilled workers in the profession of committing villainy.

"I'll give you some examples of thievery.

"The Sun's a thief, and with his great attraction he robs the vast sea. The Sun evaporates seawater.

"The Moon's an arrant thief, and she snatches her pale fire from the Sun — she reflects the light that she steals from the Sun.

"The sea's a thief, whose liquid surge — the tide — resolves the Moon into salt tears. The sea steals from the Moon what is needed to cause the tide. Since high tide involves a great amount of salty seawater, the sea must dissolve the Moon in its phases so that it becomes salty seawater.

"The Earth's a thief that feeds and breeds by a compost stolen from the excrement of animals, including men.

"Each thing's a thief.

"The laws, your curb and whip, in their rough power have unchecked theft. Who polices the police?

"Do not love yourselves. Go away. Rob one another. There's more gold. Cut throats. All whom you meet are thieves. Go to Athens, go. Break open shops; there is nothing you can steal that does not belong to thieves.

"Steal no less although I give you this. Although I give you gold, steal more gold, and may gold destroy you whatever you do! Amen."

The third bandit said, "He has almost charmed — persuaded — me not to engage in my profession, by attempting to persuade me to engage in my profession."

"He advises us to be bandits because he hates Mankind," the first bandit said, "not because he is interested in our being successful and thriving in our profession."

"I'll believe him as if he were an enemy, and I'll give over my trade," the second bandit said. "I will do the opposite of what he tells me to do, and so I will give up being a bandit."

"Let us first see peace in Athens before we reform," the first bandit said. "There is no time so miserable but a man may be true and honest and law-abiding. Since we can reform at anytime, let's reform when it's peacetime — a time when it is harder to be a successful bandit."

The bandits exited.

Flavius, Timon's old steward, arrived.

"Oh, you gods!" Flavius said. "Is yonder despised and ruinous man my lord? He is full of decay and failing! Oh, memorial and wonder of good deeds evilly bestowed! He did good deeds for evil men! What an alteration of honor has desperate need made in him! What viler thing is upon the Earth than friends who can bring the noblest minds to the basest ends! This time's custom contrasts splendidly with another time — a time when man was urged to love his enemies! May God grant that I may always love, and rather woo those who openly say they want to do mischief to me than those who pretend to be my friend and yet do mischief to me!

"He has caught me in his eye. I will present my honest grief to him, and I will continue to serve him, my lord, with my life."

He said loudly, "My dearest master!"

"Go away!" Timon replied. "Who are you?"

"Have you forgotten me, sir?" Flavius asked.

"Why do you ask me that? I have forgotten all men. Therefore, if you grant that you are a man, I have forgotten you."

"I am an honest poor servant of yours."

"Then I don't know you," Timon replied. "I have never had an honest man about me. All the servants I kept were knaves to serve food to villains."

"The gods are witnesses that never has a poor steward experienced a truer grief for his ruined lord than my eyes do for you," Flavius said.

"Are you weeping?" Timon asked. "Come closer. Then I love you, because you are a woman, and you disclaim and deny flinty, hard-hearted Mankind, whose eyes never yield tears except through lust and laughter. Pity is sleeping. These are strange times — men weep with laughing, but not with mourning!"

"I beg you to recognize and know me, my good lord," Flavius said. "I beg you to accept my grief and while this poor wealth lasts to employ me as your steward still."

The wealth referred to both the little amount of money that Flavius possessed and his still-living body.

"Did I have a steward so true and loyal, so just, and now so comforting?" Timon asked. "It almost turns my dangerous nature mild. Let me see your face. Surely, this man was born of woman."

Timon was referencing Job 14:1: *"Man that is born of woman is of short continuance and full of trouble."*

Job, like Timon, had been successful, but then had suffered. In Job 14:1, Job was saying that man, born of woman, endures a short and troubled life.

Timon continued, "Forgive my general and indiscriminate rashness, you perpetually sober gods! I do proclaim that one honest man exists — don't mistake me — there is only one honest man — no more, I pray — and he's a steward.

"How willingly would I have hated all Mankind! But you redeem yourself. Everyone except you, only you, I fell with curses.

"I think that you are more honest now than wise. For, by oppressing and betraying me, you might have more quickly gotten another job. For many acquire second masters that way: They stand upon their first lord's neck.

"But tell me truly — because I must always doubt, even when I have never been surer — isn't your kindness cunning, greedy, maybe even a kindness that is grounded in usury — a kindness like that of a rich man giving a gift and expecting in return twenty for one?"

"No, my most worthy master, in whose breast doubt and suspicion are unfortunately placed too late," Flavius said. "You should have feared false times when you feasted your 'friends.' Suspicion always comes where an estate is least.

"That which I show you, Heaven knows, is merely love, duty, and zeal to your unequalled mind, concern for your food and living, and believe me, my most honored lord, I would exchange any benefit that may come to me, either in the future or now in the present, for this one wish — that you had the power and wealth to reward me because you yourself were rich."

Showing Flavius the gold, Timon said, "Look, what you said is so! I am rich. You singly and uniquely honest man, here, take gold. Out of my misery, the gods have sent you treasure.

"Go, live rich and be happy, but with these conditions. You shall build a house distant from men. You shall hate all men, curse all men, and show charity to no men; instead, you shall let the famished flesh slide away from the bone before you relieve the hunger of the beggar. Give to dogs what you deny to men; let prisons swallow men, and let debts wither them to nothing. Let men be like blasted woods, and may diseases lick up and consume their false blood!

"And so farewell and may you thrive."

"Oh, let me stay and comfort you, my master!" Flavius pleaded.

"If you hate to be cursed, don't stay here," Timon replied. "Flee, while you are blest and free from curses. Never see another man, and let me never see you."

Taking the gold Timon had given to him, Flavius exited.

Timon went inside his cave.

CHAPTER 5
— 5.1 —

The poet and the painter arrived. Unseen by them, Timon watched them from inside his cave.

"As far as I remember, we cannot be far from where Timon lives," the painter said.

"What are we to think about him?" the poet asked. "Should we believe that the rumor is true and that he is wealthy with gold?"

"The rumor is certainly true. Alcibiades reports that Timon has gold; Phrynia and Timandra received gold from him. He likewise enriched some poor straggling soldiers with a great quantity of gold. It is said that he gave to his steward a mighty sum in gold."

The poor straggling soldiers were the bandits.

The poet said, "Then this 'bankruptcy' of his has been only a test of his friends."

"Nothing else," the painter said. "You shall see Timon a palm in Athens again, and he will flourish with the highest."

According to Psalm 92:12, "*The righteous shall flourish like a palm tree, and shall grow like a cedar in Lebanon.*"

The painter continued, "Therefore it is not amiss that we offer our friendship to him, in this supposed distress of his. It will make us appear to be honest and honorable, and it is very likely to load our purposes with what they work and travel for, if it is a just and true report that states that he is rich. We want gold, and we are likely to get some gold from Timon."

"What have you now to present to him?" the poet asked.

"Nothing at this time except for my visit," the painter said, "only I will promise him an excellent piece to be given to him later."

"I must serve him so, too," the poet said. "I will tell him of a planned work of literature that will be delivered to him in the future."

"Promising is as good as the best," the painter said. "Promising is the very fashion of the time: It opens the eyes of expectation. Performance is always the duller for its act; the finished work of art never lives up to the promise. And, except for the plainer and simpler kind of people, the keeping of a promise is quite out of the usual practice — it's just not done anymore. To promise is very courtly and fashionable. To actually do what one promised to do is a kind of will or testament that argues a great sickness in his judgment of the person who makes the will or keeps the promise. When people are very ill and therefore, in my opinion, lacking in judgment, they make wills."

Timon said to himself, "Excellent workman as you are, you cannot paint a man who is as bad as yourself!"

"I am thinking about what I shall tell Timon I have provided for him," the poet said. "It must be an impersonation of himself and his situation: a satire against the softness of prosperity, with an exposé of the infinite flatteries that follow youth and opulence."

Timon said to himself, "Must you impersonate a villain in your own work? Will you whip your own faults in other men? If you do so, I have 'gold' for you."

The poet was going to say that he would write a satire against flattery, and yet the poet was himself a flatterer. The poet had the fault that he would censure other people for having, and so it was like he was whipping people who shared his fault.

"Let's seek him, "the poet said. "Let's get to Timon before he gives all his gold away to people other than us. We would sin against our own state, when we may meet with profit, and come too late to benefit."

"That is true," the painter said. "While the day serves our goals and the Sun shines, before black-cornered night arrives, we should find what we want by freely offered light. Come."

"I'll meet you at the turn," Timon said. "I'll play your game and beat you at it. I'll pretend that you two are honest, but then I'll make clear that I know what you two really are!

"What a god is gold! He is worshipped in a baser temple than where swine feed! Gold, it is you that rigs the ship and plows the foam of the sea. You make a slave give his rich master admired reverence. Gold, may you be worshipped! And may your saints who obey only you forever be crowned with plagues!

"It is the right time for me to meet the poet and painter."

Timon came out of his cave and approached the poet and painter.

"Hail, worthy Timon!" the poet said.

"Our late noble master!" the painter said.

"Have I lived to see two honest men?" Timon said.

The poet replied, "Sir, having tasted often of your open generosity, and hearing that you had retired from society, with your friends fallen off, whose thankless natures ... oh, abhorred spirits! ... not all the whips of Heaven are large enough ... what! ... to you, whose star-like nobleness gave life and influence to their whole being!"

The poet was pretending to be so overcome with indignation that Timon's friends had abandoned him that the poet was unable to speak in complete sentences.

He continued, "I am carried away with emotion and cannot cover the monstrous bulk of this ingratitude with any size — number — of words. The words available to me are inadequate to express my feelings."

"Don't cover the monstrous bulk of this ingratitude," Timon said. "Let it go naked, so men may better see it. You who are honest, by being what you are, make them — ungrateful men — best seen and known."

"He and I have traveled in the great shower of your gifts, and sweetly felt it," the painter said.

"Yes, you are honest men," Timon said.

"We have come here to offer you our service," the painter said.

"Most honest men!" Timon said. "Why, how shall I repay you? Can you eat roots, and drink cold water?"

The poet and painter looked unhappy; they wanted gold.

Timon answered the question for them: "No."

The poet and painter said, "What we can do, we'll do, to do you service."

"You are honest men," Timon said. "You've heard that I have gold. I am sure you have. Speak the truth. You're honest men."

"It is rumored that you have gold, my noble lord," the painter said, "but that is not why my friend and I came here."

"Good honest men!" Timon said. "Painter, you draw a counterfeit the best of all the painters in Athens. You are, indeed, the best. You counterfeit most lively."

Timon's words were ambiguous. A counterfeit is a painting, or a lie. To counterfeit means to paint, or to tell a lie.

"I am only so-so, my lord," the painter said.

"What I say is true," Timon replied.

He turned to the poet and said, "And, as for your fiction, why, your verse swells with stuff so fine and smooth that you are even natural in your art."

"You are even natural in your art" is ambiguous. It can mean, "Your art is like nature because you hide the artifice in your art." But a "natural" is a "born fool." In addition, Timon was saying that the poet was gifted at creating fiction — at telling lies. And of course, "stuff" — as in stuff and nonsense — may not refer to something good. It may refer to worthless ideas.

Timon said to the poet and painter, "But, for all this, my honest-natured friends, I must say that you have a little fault. Indeed, it is not monstrous in you, nor do I wish you to take many pains to mend it."

The poet and painter said, "Please, your honor, tell us what our fault is."

"You'll take it badly," Timon replied.

"We will thank you very much for telling us, my lord."

"Will you, indeed?"

"Don't doubt that we will, worthy lord."

"Each of you trusts a scoundrel who mightily deceives you," Timon said.

"Do we, my lord?"

"Yes, and you hear him cheat, see him deceive, know his gross knavery, love him, feed him, keep him in your bosom. Yet I assure you that he is a complete villain."

"I know of no one like that, my lord," the painter said.

"Nor do I," the poet said.

"Look, both of you, I love you well," Timon said. "I'll give you gold. Rid these villains from your companies for me. Hang them or stab them, drown them in a sewer. Destroy them by some course of action, and then come to me. I'll give you gold enough."

"Name them, my lord," the poet and painter said. "Let's know who they are."

Timon said to the poet and the painter, who were standing a few feet apart, "You are standing here, and you are standing over here, and there are two of you. Each man of you is apart, all single and alone, yet an arch-villain keeps each of you company."

Timon said to the painter, "If where you are, two villains shall not be, do not come near the poet."

Timon said to the poet, "If you don't want to reside except where just one villain is, then abandon the painter."

He said to both the poet and the painter, "Leave, go packing!"

He started throwing stones at them, saying, "There's 'gold' — you came for gold, you slaves."

He said to the poet, "You have worked for me; there's payment for you. Flee!"

He said to the painter, "You are an alchemist; make gold out of that stone."

By mixing paints, the painter could make different colors — a kind of alchemy. Alchemists attempted to find the philosopher's stone, which could turn base metal into gold.

Timon shouted, "Get out, rascal dogs!"

He beat them until they ran away, and then he went into his cave.

Flavius arrived, accompanied by two Senators from Athens, which was at war with Alcibiades. Athens wanted the help of Timon — he and Alcibiades were friends and so Timon might be able to convince Alcibiades not to attack Athens.

"It is in vain that you want to speak with Timon," Flavius said, "for he is so wrapped up in himself that nothing except himself that looks like a man is friendly with him."

"Bring us to his cave," the first Senator said. "It is our duty to speak to Timon, and we have promised the Athenians that we will speak with him."

"Men are not always the same at all times alike," the second Senator said. "It was time and griefs that made him like this. Time, with a fairer hand, offering him the fortunes of his former days, may make him the man he used to be. Bring us to him, and whatever will happen, will happen."

"Here is his cave," Flavius said.

He called, "May peace and contentment be here! Lord Timon! Timon! Look out of your cave, and speak to friends. The Athenians, in the person of two of their most reverend Senators, greet you. Speak to them, noble Timon."

Timon came out of his cave and said, "You Sun, that comforts, burn!"

He said to his visitors, "Speak, and be hanged. For each true word, may you get a blister! And may each false word be as searing with pain to the root of your tongue, consuming it with speaking!"

The first Senator said, "Worthy Timon —"

Timon interrupted, "I am worthy of none but such as you, and you are worthy of Timon."

"The Senators of Athens greet you, Timon," the first Senator said.

"I thank them," Timon said, "and I would send back to them the plague, if only I could catch it for them."

The first Senator said, "Oh, forget the offenses that we ourselves are sorry for having committed against you. The Senators with one voice of love entreat you to come back to Athens. The Senators have thought about special high offices that lie vacant, but which you will best fill and possess."

The second Senator said, "The Senators confess that they have neglected you in a way that is grossly evident to all, and now the public body, which seldom admits that it made a mistake, feeling in itself a lack of and need for Timon's aid, acknowledges its own failing and mistake when it withheld aid to Timon. Therefore, the Athens Senate sent us to make to you their sorrowful admission of fault and its apology, together with recompense greater than its offence, even counting every last bit of its offense against you. Yes, the Senate offers to you even such heaps and sums of love and wealth as shall blot out for you what wrongs were theirs and write in you as if you were an account book the figures of their love, which you can read forever."

"You bewitch me with this offer," Timon said. "You surprise and overwhelm me emotionally so much that I am on the very brink of crying. Lend me a fool's heart and a woman's eyes, and I'll weep over these comforts, worthy Senators."

He was sarcastic.

The first Senator said, "Therefore, if it pleases you to return with us and to take the Captainship of our Athens — yours and ours — and defend us against Alcibiades and his army, you shall be met with thanks, you shall be legally assigned absolute power, and your good name will continue to be associated with authority; then very soon we shall drive back the wild attacks of Alcibiades, who, like a very savage boar, roots up his country's peace."

"He shakes his threatening sword against the walls of Athens," the second Senator said.

"Therefore, Timon —" the first Senator said.

Timon interrupted, "Well, sir, I will; therefore, I will, sir."

One meaning of the word "will" is "wish."

Timon continued, "This is what I will: If Alcibiades should kill my countrymen, let Alcibiades know this about Timon, that Timon cares not. But if he should sack fair Athens, and take our good, aged men by the beards, giving our holy virgins to the stain and defilement and rape of insolent, beastly, mad-brained war, then let him know, and tell him Timon speaks it, out of pity for our aged and our youth, I cannot choose but tell him, that I care not, and let him take it at the worst, for their knives care not, while you have throats to cut. As for myself, there's not a knife in the unruly camp but that I prize it and love it more than I love the most reverend throat in Athens.

"So I leave you to the protection of the propitious gods, as I would leave thieves to the protection of jailors."

Since jailors were also often executioners, such "protection" was not reassuring. And all too often, the gods seem not to be bothered by the suffering of humans.

Flavius advised the two Senators, "Don't stay and talk to Timon, for all's in vain."

Timon said, "Why, I was just now writing my epitaph; it will be seen tomorrow. My long sickness of health and living now begins to mend, and oblivion will bring me everything I want.

"Go, continue to live. May Alcibiades be your plague, may you be his plague, and may this be the case for a long time!"

"We speak in vain," the first Senator said.

"But yet I love my country," Timon said, "and I am not one who rejoices in the destruction of the community, as common rumor in the community says I do."

"That's well spoken," the first Senator said.

"Commend me to my loving countrymen —" Timon said.

"These words become your lips as they pass through them," the first Senator said.

"And they enter our ears like great conquerors enter the city through gates where people applaud," the second Senator said.

"Commend me to them," Timon repeated, "and tell them that, to ease them of their griefs, their fears of hostile strokes of war, their aches, losses, their pangs of love, with other incident throes that nature's fragile vessel — the body —

sustains during life's uncertain voyage, I will do them some kindness: I'll teach them to escape wild Alcibiades' wrath."

"I like this well," the first Senator said. "Timon will return again to Athens."

"I have a tree, which grows here beside my cave," Timon said, "that my own need requires me to cut down, and soon I will fell it. Tell my friends, tell the people of Athens, in the sequence of degree from the high class to the low class, that whoever wants to stop affliction, let him make haste and come here, before my tree has felt the axe, and hang himself. Please, give my greeting to the Athenians."

"Trouble him no further," Flavius said. "You always shall find him like this."

"Come not to me again," Timon said, "but say to the people of Athens that Timon has made his everlasting mansion upon the beach of the salty flood we call the sea, and once a day with its foaming froth the turbulent surge of waves shall cover him. There come, and let what will be written on my gravestone be your oracle:

"Lips, let sour words go by and language end.

"What is amiss may plague and infection mend!

"May graves be men's only works and death their gain!

"Sun, hide your beams! Timon has done his reign."

Timon went into his cave.

The first Senator said, "His discontent is coupled to his character, and the two cannot be separated."

"Our hope in him is dead," the second Senator said. "Let us return to Athens, and stretch to the utmost what other means and resources are left to us in our dire peril."

"We must act quickly," the first Senator said.

The two Senators headed to Athens.

Flavius may have stayed with Timon because he had learned that Timon was dying. Even if Timon wanted to die alone, someone needed to bury him after he died.

Two Senators different from the two who had visited Timon talked with a messenger at the main gate of Athens. The messenger had brought to them news concerning Alcibiades and his army.

The third Senator said, "You have taken pains to discover this information, which is painful for Athens. Are his soldiers really as numerous as you report them to be?"

"I have given to you the lowest estimate of the number of his soldiers," the messenger replied. "Besides that information, I need to tell you that the speed of his army promises that it will arrive before Athens almost immediately."

"We are in a very hazardous situation, if the other two Senators do not bring Timon back with them," the fourth Senator said.

"I met a courier, an old friend of mine," the messenger said. "Although he and I are on opposite sides in this war, yet our old friendship made itself felt, and we spoke in a friendly way together. This man was riding from Alcibiades to Timon's cave with a letter of entreaty desiring him to enlist his fellowship in the war against your city, a war that was instigated in part for his sake."

Seeing the two Senators returning from visiting Timon, the third Senator said, "Here come our brothers."

The first Senator said, "Let's have no talk about Timon; expect no help from him. The enemies' drum is heard, and the fearful and hostile movement of enemy soldiers chokes the air with dust. Let's go inside the city, and prepare. Our future is the fall, I fear; our foes are the snare."

One of Alcibiades' soldiers, seeking Timon, arrived at Timon's cave. A crude tomb was near the cave.

The soldier said to himself, "By the description I have been given, this should be the place."

He called, "Who's here? Speak! Ho!"

He said to himself, "No answer! What is this?"

He picked up a wooden board on which some words were written and read this:

"*Timon is dead, who has outstretched his life span.*

"*Some beast read this; there does not live a man.*"

Timon was cynical to the end. Whoever would read this would have to be a beast, for all men are beasts and are not men.

The soldier said to himself, "Timon is dead, for sure; and this is his grave."

Something was written on the tomb. Apparently, what was written on the wooden board was Timon's epitaph, or a first draft of Timon's epitaph.

The soldier said to himself, "What's written on this tomb is in a language I cannot read; I'll write on my wax table what is written. Our Captain has skill with all languages. As an interpreter, he is aged — experienced — although he is young in days.

"By this time he's arrived at Athens, whose fall is the goal of his ambition."

In front of the walls of Athens, Alcibiades stood with his soldiers and trumpeters.

He told his trumpeters, "Blow and announce to this cowardly and lascivious town our terrifying approach."

The sound of the trumpets announced the request for a parley between the opposing sides.

Some Athenian Senators looked over the walls of Athens.

Alcibiades said to them, "Until now you have gone on and filled the time with all kinds of licentious acts, making your wills the scope of justice. To you, what is just is whatever will give you what you want. Until now I and people like me who have stepped within the shadow of your power have wandered with our arms crossed — not threatening you with weapons — and we have complained about our suffering in vain. Now the time is ripe, when the suppressed courage in us strongly cries, 'No more.' Now you breathless wrongdoers shall sit and pant in your great chairs of ease, and you short-winded insolent men shall break your wind with fear and horrid flight."

A chair of ease can be a comfortable position of high office, or it can be a comfortable chair that a flatulent high-ranking man would sit in.

The first Senator said, "Noble and young Alcibiades, when your first grievances were only a mere notion and unimportant, before you had power or we had cause to fear, we sent to you, offering to give balm to your rages and offering to wipe out our ungrateful acts with acts of friendship above their quantity."

The second Senator said, "So also did we woo transformed Timon to our city's friendship by sending him a humble message and by promising him resources. We were not all unkind, nor do we all deserve the indiscriminate stroke of war."

The first Senator said, "These walls of ours were not erected by the hands of those from whom you have received your griefs, nor are they such that these great towers, monuments, and public buildings should fall because some particular men who are at fault are in them."

The second Senator said, "Nor are those men still living who were the instigators of your exile. They were ashamed because they lacked intelligence when they exiled you, and that excess of shame has broken their hearts and killed them. March, noble lord, into our city with your banners spread. By decimation, and a tithed death — one out of every ten men to die — if your desire for revenge hungers for that cannibalistic food that nature loathes — take you the destined tenth, and by the hazard of the spotted die let die those who are spotted with sin."

The first Senator said, "Not everyone has offended you. It is not fair to take revenge on those who have not offended you for the sins of those who have offended you.

"Crimes, like lands, are not inherited."

This is an interesting sentence. Most likely, the first Senator had misspoken and meant to say, "Crimes, unlike lands, are not inherited." Certainly, lands are left to heirs in wills. Or perhaps the first Senator meant that land can never really be owned, for the land was here long before the "owner" was born and will be here long after the "owner" has died. And perhaps the first Senator was also saying that if lands cannot be inherited, then crimes certainly cannot. A crime is immaterial, while land is material. If a material thing cannot be inherited, then certainly an immaterial thing cannot be inherited.

The first Senator continued, "So then, dear countryman, bring into Athens your ranks of soldiers, but leave outside the city your rage. Spare your Athenian cradle and those kin of yours who in the bluster of your wrath must fall along with those who have offended. Like a shepherd, approach the fold and cull the infected forth, but kill not all together."

The second Senator said, "Whatever it is you want, it is better for you to use your smile to get it rather than hew with your sword to get it."

The first Senator said, "Simply set your foot against our gates that are fortified with ramps of earth, and the gates shall open as long as you will metaphorically send your gentle heart first to say you shall enter as a friend."

The second Senator said, "Throw your glove, or any other pledge of your honor, to let us know that you will use the wars to redress the wrongs done to you and not to destroy us all. If you do this, all your soldiers shall make their harbor in our town, until we have carried out your full desire and redressed the wrongs done to you."

Alcibiades threw down his glove and said, "Then there's my glove. Descend, and open your gates, which I have not attacked. Those enemies of Timon's and my own enemies whom you yourselves shall pick out for reproof shall fall and no more, and to appease your fears with my more noble purpose, not a soldier of mine shall go outside the boundary of his quarters, or offend the stream of regular justice in your city's boundaries. If any soldier of mine does this, he shall be delivered to your public courts and pay the heaviest penalty."

The two Senators said, "This is most nobly spoken."

"Descend, and keep your words," Alcibiades said.

The two Senators descended and opened the gates.

The soldier who had been sent to see Timon arrived and said to Alcibiades, "My noble general, Timon is dead. He has been entombed upon the very edge of the sea, and on his gravestone was written this inscription, which I copied onto a wax tablet and brought away. The soft impression of the letters on the wax will reveal to you what my poor ignorance was unable to interpret."

Alcibiades translated and read the inscription out loud:

"*Here lies a wretched corpse, of wretched soul bereft.*

"*Seek not my name. May a plague consume you wicked wretches who are still left!*

"*Here lie I, Timon, who, when I was alive, all living men did hate.*

"*Pass by and curse your fill, but pass and stay not here your gait.*"

Alcibiades said, "These words, Timon, well express in your epitaph your latter spirits and mood. Though you hated in us our human griefs, scorned our brain's flow — our droplets, our tears, that fall from parsimonious human nature — yet your rich imagination taught you to make the sea-god Neptune's vast sea weep always during its high tide on your low grave, on faults forgiven. Death forgives faults.

"Noble Timon is dead. We will speak more about his memory soon.

"Bring me into your city, and I will use the olive branch as well as my sword. I will make war breed peace, and make peace stop war. I will make each prescribe to the other as if they were each other's physician."

He ordered, "Let our drums strike," and he and the others marched into the city.

NOTES

— 4.3 —

• This is a quotation from Francis Bacon about a belief that he rejects:

*Wherefore there are axioms, or rather certain conceits, which, received by philosophers, and transferred to astronomy, and unfortunately being credited, have corrupted the science. Our rejection of them will be simple, as well as our judgment upon them; for it is not suitable to waste precious time on silly refutations. The first of these is, that **all things above the moon inclusively are incorruptible**; and in no degree or form whatever do they undergo new beginnings or changes; of which it has been said elsewhere, that it is a fond and silly saying.*

Bold added.

Source: Francis Bacon, *The Works of Francis Bacon* (1884) *Volume 1*.djvu/548

<https://tinyurl.com/y43xycvu>.

• The quotation from the sixteenth-century *Shiltei Hagiborim* by R. Joshua Boaz comes from this book:

Windows onto Jewish Legal Culture: Fourteen Exploratory Essays, edited by Hanina Ben-Menahem, Arye Edrei, Neil S. Hecht. Page 127.

• For what it's worth, I found this paragraph online:

The Voodoo religion makes wide use of feathers. Pillow magic is the practice of placing objects into the pillow of a person to cause wasting sickness and even death. Feather pillows are the best type to use because of feathers' magical properties. By using secret spells the "Voodoo" can cause bird or animal monsters to take shape out of the pillow feathers. It will grow slowly and only at night. When it is completely formed the person who has been sleeping on the pillow will die.

The above paragraph is from the May 2012 article "Strange Superstitions About Feathers" at <http://tinyurl.com/h88qwpp>. This is the site for *Nature Center Magazine.*

I also found this paragraph online:

PIGEONS: a lone white pigeon perching on a chimney is said to be a death omen. For quite a long time when feather beds were popular, it was claimed that pigeon feathers in such a bed only prolonged the agonies of someone dying, and consequently any pillow or mattress containing them was invariably removed from a sick-room.

Source: SUPERSTITIONS and OLD WIVES' TALES
©winnie caw 2002
http://www.whimsy.org.uk/superstitions.html
• I retold the Aesop's fable about the fox, lion, and stag from this book:

Aesop's Fables: A New Translation by V. S. Vernon Jones. With an Introduction by G. K. Chesterton and Illustrations by Arthur Rackham. 1912 Edition. Pp. 212-214.

Aesop's Fables: A New Translation is available at Project Gutenberg: http://www.gutenberg.org/ebooks/11339
• I adapted the Aesop's fable about the ass, fox, and lion so that the ass accused the fox of treachery.
• I adapted the Aesop's fable about a wolf and a lamb so that it was about a fox and a lamb.

Appendix A: About the Author

It was a dark and stormy night. Suddenly a cry rang out, and on a hot summer night in 1954, Josephine, wife of Carl Bruce, gave birth to a boy — me. Unfortunately, this young married couple allowed Reuben Saturday, Josephine's brother, to name their first-born. Reuben, aka "The Joker," decided that Bruce was a nice name, so he decided to name me Bruce Bruce. I have gone by my middle name — David — ever since.

Being named Bruce David Bruce hasn't been all bad. Bank tellers remember me very quickly, so I don't often have to show an ID. It can be fun in charades, also. When I was a counselor as a teenager at Camp Echoing Hills in Warsaw, Ohio, a fellow counselor gave the signs for "sounds like" and "two words," then she pointed to a bruise on her leg twice. Bruise Bruise? Oh yeah, Bruce Bruce is the answer!

Uncle Reuben, by the way, gave me a haircut when I was in kindergarten. He cut my hair short and shaved a small bald spot on the back of my head. My mother wouldn't let me go to school until the bald spot grew out again.

Of all my brothers and sisters (six in all), I am the only transplant to Athens, Ohio. I was born in Newark, Ohio, and have lived all around Southeastern Ohio. However, I moved to Athens to go to Ohio University and have never left.

At Ohio U, I never could make up my mind whether to major in English or Philosophy, so I got a bachelor's degree with a double major in both areas, then I added a Master of Arts degree in English and a Master of Arts degree in Philosophy. Yes, I have my MAMA degree.

Currently, and for a long time to come (I eat fruits and veggies), I am spending my retirement writing books such as *Nadia Comaneci: Perfect 10*, *The Funniest People in Dance*, *Homer's* Iliad: *A Retelling in Prose*, and *William Shakespeare's* Othello: *A Retelling in Prose*.

By the way, my sister Brenda Kennedy writes romances such as *A New Beginning* and *Shattered Dreams*.

Appendix B: Some Books by David Bruce

Retellings of a Classic Work of Literature

Arden of Faversham: *A Retelling*

Ben Jonson's The Alchemist: *A Retelling*

Ben Jonson's The Arraignment, or Poetaster: *A Retelling*

Ben Jonson's Bartholomew Fair: *A Retelling*

Ben Jonson's The Case is Altered: *A Retelling*

Ben Jonson's Catiline's Conspiracy: *A Retelling*

Ben Jonson's The Devil is an Ass: *A Retelling*

Ben Jonson's Epicene: *A Retelling*

Ben Jonson's Every Man in His Humor: *A Retelling*

Ben Jonson's Every Man Out of His Humor: *A Retelling*

Ben Jonson's The Fountain of Self-Love, or Cynthia's Revels: *A Retelling*

Ben Jonson's The Magnetic Lady, or Humors Reconciled: *A Retelling*

Ben Jonson's The New Inn, or The Light Heart: *A Retelling*

Ben Jonson's Sejanus' Fall: *A Retelling*

Ben Jonson's The Staple of News: *A Retelling*

Ben Jonson's A Tale of a Tub: *A Retelling*

Ben Jonson's Volpone, or the Fox: *A Retelling*

Christopher Marlowe's Complete Plays: Retellings

Christopher Marlowe's Dido, Queen of Carthage: *A Retelling*

Christopher Marlowe's Doctor Faustus: *Retellings of the 1604 A-Text and of the 1616 B-Text*

Christopher Marlowe's Edward II: *A Retelling*

Christopher Marlowe's The Massacre at Paris: *A Retelling*

Christopher Marlowe's The Rich Jew of Malta: *A Retelling*

Christopher Marlowe's Tamburlaine, Parts 1 and 2: *Retellings*

Dante's Divine Comedy: *A Retelling in Prose*

Dante's Inferno: *A Retelling in Prose*

Dante's Purgatory: *A Retelling in Prose*

Dante's Paradise: *A Retelling in Prose*

The Famous Victories of Henry V: *A Retelling*

From the Iliad *to the* Odyssey: *A Retelling in Prose of Quintus of Smyrna's* Posthomerica

George Chapman, Ben Jonson, and John Marston's Eastward Ho! *A Retelling*

George Peele's The Arraignment of Paris: *A Retelling*

George Peele's The Battle of Alcazar: *A Retelling*

George's Peele's David and Bathsheba, and the Tragedy of Absalom: *A Retelling*

George Peele's Edward I: *A Retelling*

George Peele's The Old Wives' Tale: *A Retelling*

George-a-Greene: *A Retelling*

William Shakespeare's 1 Henry IV, aka Henry IV, Part 1: *A Retelling in Prose*

William Shakespeare's 2 Henry IV, aka Henry IV, Part 2: *A Retelling in Prose*

William Shakespeare's 1 Henry VI, aka Henry VI, Part 1: *A Retelling in Prose*

William Shakespeare's 2 Henry VI, aka Henry VI, Part 2: *A Retelling in Prose*

William Shakespeare's 3 Henry VI, aka Henry VI, Part 3: *A Retelling in Prose*

William Shakespeare's All's Well that Ends Well: *A Retelling in Prose*

William Shakespeare's Antony and Cleopatra: *A Retelling in Prose*

William Shakespeare's As You Like It: *A Retelling in Prose*

William Shakespeare's The Comedy of Errors: *A Retelling in Prose*

William Shakespeare's Coriolanus: *A Retelling in Prose*

William Shakespeare's Cymbeline: *A Retelling in Prose*

William Shakespeare's Hamlet: *A Retelling in Prose*

William Shakespeare's Henry V: *A Retelling in Prose*

William Shakespeare's Henry VIII: *A Retelling in Prose*

William Shakespeare's Julius Caesar: *A Retelling in Prose*

William Shakespeare's King John: *A Retelling in Prose*

William Shakespeare's King Lear: *A Retelling in Prose*

William Shakespeare's Love's Labor's Lost: *A Retelling in Prose*

William Shakespeare's Macbeth: *A Retelling in Prose*

William Shakespeare's Measure for Measure: *A Retelling in Prose*

William Shakespeare's The Merchant of Venice: *A Retelling in Prose*

William Shakespeare's The Merry Wives of Windsor: *A Retelling in Prose*

William Shakespeare's A Midsummer Night's Dream: *A Retelling in Prose*

William Shakespeare's Much Ado About Nothing: *A Retelling in Prose*

William Shakespeare's Othello: *A Retelling in Prose*

William Shakespeare's Pericles, Prince of Tyre: *A Retelling in Prose*

William Shakespeare's Richard II: *A Retelling in Prose*

William Shakespeare's Richard III: *A Retelling in Prose*

William Shakespeare's Romeo and Juliet: *A Retelling in Prose*

William Shakespeare's The Taming of the Shrew: *A Retelling in Prose*

William Shakespeare's The Tempest: *A Retelling in Prose*

William Shakespeare's Timon of Athens: *A Retelling in Prose*

William Shakespeare's Titus Andronicus: *A Retelling in Prose*

William Shakespeare's Troilus and Cressida: *A Retelling in Prose*

William Shakespeare's Twelfth Night: *A Retelling in Prose*

William Shakespeare's The Two Gentlemen of Verona: *A Retelling in Prose*

William Shakespeare's The Two Noble Kinsmen: *A Retelling in Prose*

William Shakespeare's The Winter's Tale: *A Retelling in Prose*